A TRAIL OF BLOOD ON THE SNOW

A TRAIL OF BLOOD ON THE SNOW

A *BARBICAN FIRST* BY

SAM LEE

Published by Barbican Press

Copyright © Sam Lee, 2025

Registered office: 1 Ashenden Road, London E5 0DP

www.barbicanpress.com
@barbicanpress1

A CIP catalogue for this book is available from the British Library

ISBN: 978-1-909954-28-1
Ebook ISBN: 978-1-909954-29-8

Sam Lee is a 28-year-old writer from Canada, but she has called the Dominican Republic home since she was six. At age eight she started an all-girl rock band, *Crush*, opening for her father's band across island gigs. In her pre-teens she started playing bass and writing her own material, now touring globally as a bass player/singer in the alt-rock band *Still Eighteen*. Other passions are snowboarding, or making tiny cactuses out of clay for no apparent reason. *A Trail of Blood on the Snow* is her first published novel.

For Chris, for your unconditional love and unwavering support, and for curating books and films that have greatly inspired my writing. Thank you for believing so much in this book, and for all of your insight. You are one of my favorite artists and people in this world.

For my parents, who have taught me how to hold onto a dream. You supported my writing dream for a decade and never once thought I was delusional, which is quite the feat. You are the best parents in the world. I love you.

"Even when they desert hell, men do so only to reconstruct it elsewhere."

EMIL CIORAN, *The Trouble with Being Born*

One

I am unhappy with life. I am very, very bored with it. When I met my wife we were sixteen and her eyes were sparkly and on our first date, we went to a diner and shared a banana split. She had eyeliner on and dangly earrings and she smiled a lot. It was like she tricked me into thinking I'd be happy with her for the rest of my life, because now I'm forty-one and she's forty-one and we're only halfway through this whole shit show and happiness is nowhere to be found.

I've looked for happiness in the eyes of my fat daughter, but all she does is stare at her cell phone screen and wear whore makeup to school and mutter unintelligible things once in a while when I ask her how she's doing. I've looked for happiness out on the open road, staring out at the vast open sky, but it only reminds me that I spend over half my life stuck in a van, delivering bag after bag of potato chips, abetting America's obesity epidemic. I've looked for happiness in my bedroom, but my wife and I only have sex about twice a year and we never cuddle anymore. I swear we were in love once, when we weren't chubby and depressed, but now we're strangers. We're more roommates than soul mates.

My wife looks bad now. She used to be almost pretty. There used to be a lot of life in those brown eyes. But now her face is falling, her jowls like a bulldog's, and she's got more frown lines than smile lines. I don't look much better. My hair is falling out and I'm fat and I'm short and I'm hairy. I've never been a looker. My mother always said I was. "You've got the most beautiful eyes," she used to say. "You've got the kind of eyes that drive girls wild." And alright, maybe my eyes were fine but who's got ugly eyes, anyway? The rest of me was pretty ugly. I have this long, crooked nose like a tree branch in search of the sun and a bad haircut and a limp. When I was five years old, I fell out of a tree and my leg's never been the same since. Now I drag it with me everywhere like a separate entity.

Kids used to call me Gimpy. On the playground, no one wanted to play with me. In gym class, no one wanted me on their team. "Gimpy's limp will slow us down," that's what the other boys used to say, the tall ones with white teeth and strong arms. "Gimpy sucks at sports. Gimpy sucks at everything." I used to walk with my head hung, to such excess that I grew to be a bit of a hunchback. The kids made fun of me for that too. And I used to do awful bad in school, and in the seventh grade, I got held back. That made my mother cry, and that made my dad pretty mad because we both hated it when my mother cried and I think my dad's thought of me as a disappointment ever since.

Even before he thought I was a disappointment, my dad always loved my older sister more than me. My sister was one of those real Italian divas who clacked their gum and wore a leather jacket and stayed out late. She was always with a new guy, riding around on the back of his motorcycle or sneaking into bars with a fake ID. She was so cool. I used to follow her around sometimes because her life was like watching a really cool movie. Once I saw her having sex with some bearded college guy through his dorm room window. I didn't mean to look because that was awful private, but then I couldn't look away and my dick got hard and I was glad no one was around to see me standing there at that window stroking my hard dick.

I was sixteen when that happened and that same year a new Italian family moved into the neighborhood. My mother loved them right away on account of them being Italian like us. My mom made me bring them over some cannolis with my sister. We rang the doorbell and my sister was blowing her bangs out of her eyes and studying her nails and huffing and puffing a lot and looking bored and cool in the way she always did and then the door opened and it was the mother, who had a lot of wrinkles, and then there was Angela behind her. Angela had freckles on her nose and brown hair and she was curvy and her face was half plain and half pretty and she had a great rack. I remember thinking of my sister blowing that bearded guy and how I'd like Angela to do that to me.

They took the cannolis and told us to thank our mother and then they came over for dinner the following week and Angela and I sat across from each other and I was sweating something awful and I remember I went to the bathroom and stuffed tissues in my armpits to keep the sweat from showing through. I liked Angela a lot after that night, even though we didn't say much, and sometimes I would watch her through her window, talking on the phone or reading a book. I liked the way she bit her bottom lip when she read, and how she paced around her room when she talked on her phone. Once I saw her change her shirt. I saw her bra. I got hard again, even though it wasn't a very racy kind of bra.

I started to take pictures of Angela because she started going to the same school as me. I had lots of pictures of her, pictures of her on the bleachers eating lunch, and pictures of her in the hallways. Luckily, I never got caught. I was awful discreet about it all. I was good at being discreet, invisible.

"You can't just be invisible forever," my sister told me once. She was on her way to a party and she looked good, her boobs all pushed up to the sky. I could never believe that she was my sister. She could have been a movie star.

I was sitting at my desk doing some homework. "What do you mean?" I said.

She rolled her eyes. She was always rolling her eyes, like the whole world was wasting her time. "You're sixteen, Rex. Don't you want to get laid?" I just shrugged, even though I would have given my right arm to get laid. She rolled her eyes again and leaned her weight against the doorframe. "I see the way you look at Angela. I know you spy on her, you little perv. You're not that ugly, you know." She took a step forward and her heels clacked on the floor. She licked her fingers and messed up the front of my hair. "There that's better," she said. "And stop wearing those jeans. They're terrible. Get some better jeans."

"Okay," I said because my sister never really acknowledged me and I felt lucky that someone so cool was talking to me, even if she was family, and I thought I'd better listen to whatever she said. That week, I bought some new jeans and some hair gel, and the kinds of shirts that cool guys wear. I even got a nice new haircut. I did look a little better, but I still had a huge ass nose and a limp. One day, Angela was taking out the trash at the same time I was getting the mail and we were right across the street from each other. Usually, I would have hung my head like the hunchback I was and not said a word, but I was feeling a little confident because I'd just watched an Elvis Presley movie so I said "hi" and she said "hi" and I remember I could hear my blood rushing in my ears and I wished I'd put some tissues under my armpits again but I still tried to be Elvis Presley cool and I said "wanna go out sometime?" and to my surprise, she said "sure" and then I walked back inside my house and I didn't sleep that whole night.

That Friday at 7 p.m. I took her to a diner. I didn't have much to say and she didn't either, but she looked good and I looked about as good as I could make myself look and we shared that banana split and I kissed her after and she let me. It was the best night of my life.

We got married when we were twenty-two. We felt really young and we were having sex all the time and laughing at everything. Angela was a really bad cook and she was always breaking things. She would laugh whenever a plate or glass would break. She had a really nice laugh, the kind of laugh that helped you forget about anything bad that had ever happened to you.

Our daughter was all pink and squished in looking when she came out. I loved her right away and I never wanted anything bad to happen to her. I got so scared of everything after she was born. I didn't like carrying her anywhere in case I tripped. She was my favorite thing in the world. She was always laughing and smiling that gummy smile. She made everything more fun and more interesting like you were seeing the world with brand new eyes and it didn't look half as bad as you would have thought, but then I got a job as a delivery driver and I was gone all the time and it was like every time I got back from driving she grew a foot and I missed her first words and first steps and first period and then she was this whole dull, morbidly obese person who I barely even knew. She has three chins this year. Last year, she had two. Sometimes I have these nightmares about her blowing up and up like a balloon until she bursts apart, the walls covered in spaghetti splatters of blood and brain pieces.

I blame Angela for the way she is. She always lets Tiffany do whatever she wants. Say whatever she wants. *Most certainly eat whatever she wants*. What I hate most is Tiffany's friends, slutty little teenagers with blank stares and tight jeans who talk the same and dress the same and think the same. Girls like that are the cancer of the earth.

We wouldn't dare say it, but I think Ang and I are disappointed in Tiff. I think a lot of parents are disappointed in

6

their kids, and it's not their kids' fault or anything. They're disappointed because having kids didn't save them. Didn't color their lives magical. I think a lot of people who have kids never really wanted kids, they wanted a miracle.

I'd like to talk about deep stuff like that with Angela, but I don't know how to talk to her about deep stuff these days because it's like I can't find her anymore. It's like she's lost beneath layers of sorrow and flab. I'd like to work on our marriage and sometimes I rub her shoulders at night but really, I'm just too tired to try and fix anything, especially when I get home from driving all day, and I don't have the energy to try to resurrect whatever we once had. Sadly, I can barely remember what that was anymore.

Sometimes, when Ang and I sit across the table from each other at dinnertime I picture the table growing like Pinocchio's nose, stretching on and on, and when Angela says something like "pass the bread" it sounds like its underwater because that's how far away she seems.

Two

I see his daughter first. She picks up a bottle of green juice and skips over to her mother, her ponytail swinging. Her mother is standing in the gas station store lineup, waiting to pay at the cash. She's beautiful and fit and she has on one of those real preppy outfits that rich people wear, complete with a sweater tied around her neck. Her hand is lying on her son's shoulder, a freckled thirteen-ish-year-old in a light blue polo shirt. It makes me sick how happy and good-looking they all are. It's like they're filming a commercial.

I've already paid for my gas station donut and coffee and I'm walking back to my van when I see Max Adams putting gas into his BMW, the sun sparkling off of his sparkly white teeth. I can see my short, fat reflection in the BMW's glossy black paint, my balding head and pot belly. Max Adams has a sweater tied around his neck too and he's wearing khaki shorts and boat shoes, and a dark blue polo shirt. Those shiny, happy people in the gas station store must be his family.

His preppy wife and preppy kids walk out of the store and over to Max Adams' BMW. His wife hands him a green juice. "Thanks, honey," he says and kisses her on the cheek, and I picture them having sex in some beautiful four-poster bed in a master bedroom that overlooks the water, and even in her white preppy mom pants, I can tell that her ass is that of a twenty-year-old's.

"Can I help you?" Max Adams asks me, taking off his sunglasses to glare at me. I guess I've been staring at them for too long. I stand there stock-still. Seeing his eyes makes me go cold. He places a protective arm on his wife's back and ushers her into the car. "Come on honey," he says. "Let's get going."

His perfect wife and perfect kids get into his perfect car and drive away. And I get in my van and follow.

They're going camping. I can tell by the tents in the back of the BMW, as well as the bright orange canoe strapped to the roof. I don't know why I'm following them. I'm in some sort of a trance. I just can't believe I saw Max Adams again. He hasn't recognized me, of that I'm sure. I was standing pretty far away. I want him to recognize me. I want to see the horror that comes across his face when he does.

After following them for forty minutes or so, they turn into a campsite so I do too. I watch them while they pitch their tents, laughing and horsing around, the freckled boy making faces at his sister, the sister pushing him down on the ground in a joking way, Max Adams smiling.

When they're nearly done setting up, I get out of my van, which I've parked not too far away, and make my way over to them. "Hey," I call out.

Max Adams spins around, takes off his sunglasses again. "Did you follow us here?" he says. He gives his wife a worried look.

"Come with me kids," his wife says. "Let's get in the car."

The girl child stares at me, frightened, then looks away. The boy makes a beeline for the BMW. I take a few steps toward Max Adams. He puffs out his chest, but I can see fear in his blue perfect eyes and that makes me happy. I keep taking steps toward him, not saying anything. He backs up when I'm only a couple of feet away. "Sir, please get away from us," he says. I take another step forward. I'm so close that I can smell his fancy aftershave. His Adam's apple bobs. He takes a step back, his boat shoes nearly tripping over a tree stub. I love how he fears me. I'm drunk on it, but I know I have to speak, and fast before he bolts to his car. "It's Rex," I say. "Rex Constanzo."

He looks like he's seen a ghost and he probably thinks he is seeing a ghost for a minute because he probably thought I'd hung myself from my bedroom ceiling a long time ago after what he did to me. His Adam's apple bobs again. He glances over his shoulder, then down at those leather boat shoes. He can't look at me. It's hard to look at him too, hard to look into those evil, glittering eyes. Those eyes that bring back everything I've tried and failed to forget.

"I don't know you, sir," he says, his gaze wandering all around, sweat beading his forehead. "Please leave us be."

"My apologies," I say, my tone fake-friendly. "You're the spitting image of an old high school friend."

"No worries," he says, but I can tell he's full of worries, and that he doesn't buy my bluff. He backs up slowly, then skids around and walks quickly to his car, like a sissy. His wife is already in the driver's seat, and they speed away, leaving me alone with their half-made tents and the sickly-sweet smell of Max Adams' aftershave.

He remembers me. He remembers the screaming and the blood on the snow. He remembers everything; I can tell.

Three

As soon as the Adams' BMW turns the corner, I race to my car in the campsite parking lot and drive back onto the highway. It's a long stretch of highway without any turns for a while, and I can see the bright orange canoe strapped to Max Adams' BMW way in the distance, shining like a tiny sun. I want to let Max Adams go, let the past go—that part of me go—but I'm still in that trance, and the canoe is taunting me, taunting me just like Max Adams used to taunt me, calling my name. So I obey. So I follow.

Max Adams' house is as beautiful as I'd expected it to be and it's only about twenty minutes from mine. I can't believe I've spent my whole adult life living twenty minutes away from Max Adams and never knew it. The BMW pulls into their drive-way, and Max Adams and his perfect wife and perfect kids get out and head inside.

I drive past them and park around the block. Their prop-erty is bordered by a forest on one side, and I walk through it to reach their house. When the forest ends, I creep carefully up to the nearest window and look inside. Max Adams sets his camping backpack down on the kitchen floor. He opens the fridge and gets out a green juice, the same brand as the one from the gas station. It looks disgusting. He takes out another three of the same bottles and passes them to the rest of his family. They exit the kitchen and step out of view. I hear the sound of the doors to their back deck sliding open. I crawl closer to the deck, hiding behind bushes by the railings.

They sit on spotless white chairs and stare out at their expansive view of Lake Michigan as it glistens in the sun. They drink their disgusting green drinks. I guess that's why all of them look like they're glowing, capable of running a marathon at the drop of a hat. The girl child is probably about nine, and her arms are sinewy and strong, an athlete's body, like she takes dance classes or does gymnastics. Her mother has got the same kind of body, but more womanly, with a pert ass and perky breasts. Maybe if Tiffany and Angela and I started drinking those green juices and exercising we wouldn't be so fat and dead inside.

I'm so close to them now. There's no window, no walls between us anymore. I try to keep my breathing quiet as I listen to their conversation.

They talk about nothing interesting. The kids talk about school and Max Adams talks about work and his wife talks about how she's going to the spa next week. They all bore me to tears, but whenever I hear Max Adams' voice I shudder and it takes me right back to that day. *You can't run Gimpy, not with that limp. You can't run away.*

I thought they'd mention me. Talk about how I ruined their camping plans, but they never did. I guess they'd exhausted that subject in the car. Max Adams most likely had them convinced that it was nothing but a weird run-in with some washed-up schizophrenic.

It was torture to hear Max Adams' voice, to see how well he'd turned out, how happy they all seemed. I don't know why I was subjecting myself to it. I guess I want to hurt him. I want to hurt Max Adams like he's hurt me. I want revenge and I want it bad.

And I decide right then and there that I'm going to get it.

Four

I had a pretty good childhood. I got to ride my bike around our little neighborhood, and on Sundays, we would go on Sunday drives. My mom would pack snacks and fill coolers with sodas and we would drive somewhere pretty and set out a picnic blanket and look out over Lake Michigan or feed ducks in the park or something. I had a friend that lived next door. His name was Steve and he was even uglier and dorkier than me. He had acne and breathing problems and too many allergies to count. He was freakishly thin and there was always food stuck in his braces. Steve was pretty boring. He was kind of like talking to a wall, but I felt sorry for him so I'd let him go biking with me and sometimes he would come over for dinner.

My sister always had lots of friends, pretty girls with great asses. Steve and I would loiter around them from the time we were ten, spying on them with binoculars when they were tanning at the public pool, offering to put sunscreen on their backs. "Get out of here, pervs!" my sister would say, but no matter how pretty or cool my sister's friends were, no one was as pretty or cool as her. She made sure of that.

And that's sort of how it felt with Steve. I felt almost cool compared to him, even with my limp. By the time I was eleven,

I'd kissed two girls, one at the school dance and one at a birthday party. I felt like Casanova compared to Steve, who I reckon still hasn't gotten laid to this day.

Before Max Adams moved to town, I had it good, easy, even if I was born ugly and talentless. I was always jealous of my sister, who has wanted to be a fashion designer since she was a little kid. She was always making clothes in her room, her sewing machine whirring past many midnights. She really had something to live for, something that made her excited to get out of bed in the morning. I never really had anything like that. I guess I was excited about Angela for a while, and Tiff after she was born, but that excitement didn't last. I've been depressed for about as long as I can remember, but since running into Max Adams I feel brand new.

Max Adams made something break in me all those years ago. It's like he broke me in half. That's the only way I can describe it. And I'm not talking about the name-calling or even the wedgies. That I could handle, was used to. I'm talking about that day in the forest. But I won't get into that. I can't. It makes me feel like my brain is bleeding and that blood is coming out of my eyes and mouth and nose and ears. I was sixteen when what happened happened and I've never been the same since. It was like all the colors went away. And I got weird in the head. I started thinking different. I went a bit crazy, I think.

I didn't tell anybody. To this day nobody knows, not even Angela. But I started acting really strange afterward. Sometimes,

I don't even remember being somewhere or doing something. It's like I'm somewhere else all the time, somewhere where I don't have to feel anything. I think that maybe Max Adams killed me that day, that he stole my soul or something because I don't feel like me, I really don't.

Once when I was sixteen, my sister snuck out on the back of some guy's motorcycle to go dancing and when she came back it was three in the morning and I was standing out in the snow on our front lawn just staring at the moon. She called my name a few times and I tried to speak but I just couldn't. She started shaking my shoulders and then it was like my consciousness snapped back into my body like Lego and I realized that I was really cold out there in the snow in nothing but my pajamas and that I was shivering. "Rex, how long have you been out here?" my sister said. I just looked at her. I remember this terrible worry in her brown-golden eyes. She put a hand on my back. "Come on," she said. "Let's get you inside."

Five

I stay there spying on Max Adams and his family in their beautiful house until it's dark outside. Through a window, I watch them eat roasted chicken and roasted potatoes and pumpkin pie. After the kids head upstairs to sleep, Max Adams and his wife sit on the back deck. They drink wine and hold hands and stare at the stars. An hour later, they're off to bed. I can't see them when they're upstairs but I stay there on their property for a while anyway and look out at the water and think about things. I think that maybe I should bring Tiffany and Angela out to the water and maybe I should buy them those disgusting green drinks too. Maybe we'd be happy then, happy like Max Adams and his family.

When it's really late, I hear the door open to the back deck. It's Max Adams in pajamas and a housecoat. He walks down the deck stairs toward the water. On silent feet, I follow him. He looks out at the night and draws in a few deep breaths. He starts crying, bawling his pretty blue eyes out, his whole body shaking. I can't believe it and I think it's amazing that beautiful rich people who seem so happy can find things to cry about and a part of me wonders if he's crying about what he did to me. If I did what he did, I'd be crying for the rest of my life.

The whole world is fucked, I think as I walk away, back toward my shitty car and my shitty house and life. *The whole world is fucked and no one is happy.*

Six

The whole next day I think of Max Adams. Being a delivery driver gives you a lot of time to think. I hate Max Adams so much that I want to kill him, but that wouldn't be enough. I want him to die a thousand deaths, a million even.

I remember it was so peaceful in the forest on the day my life got ruined. It was cold but not too cold and it was sunny too. Everything was feeling pretty Christmassy because everyone had Christmas lights strung up around their houses. I always cut through this little forest on my walk to and from school. It wasn't even that much of a shortcut, I just liked being out in nature and breathing in the fresh air and seeing all the birds and squirrels.

It wasn't until a twig snapped that I knew I was being followed. "Wait up, Gimpy." It was Max Adams' evil voice. I remember my muscles tensing up and my guts falling to my knees it seemed. I started running but my leg made me slow. He started laughing and the laughter kept getting closer and closer until I could feel him right behind me, could feel his hot breath in my ear. *You can't run Gimpy, not with that limp. You can't run away.*

I shake my head around like that could make the memory fall out of my ear. I focus on the road and driving. I think about Tiffany and how maybe we can start doing something together, like join some sort of class or something. Maybe we can learn guitar together, or make a birdhouse. Maybe she isn't too late for saving. And I'm gonna buy Angela flowers and tonight, I'll wash her hair for her in the bathtub like I did when we first moved in together.

In the evening, I make dinner before Angela gets home from her shift at the hospital. Tiffany keeps watching me from the living room couch, snarling up at me over her phone, her face lit up by the light of the screen. "Can you even cook, dad?" she says.

I laugh. "I'm gonna try. Why don't you come help me?"

She sighs. "I'm busy, dad."

A few minutes goes by and all you can hear are her fingers typing away on her phone and the almost-silent sound of me grating cheese for the lasagna. "Come on, Tiff, remember when you were little and you had that pretend kitchen? You would spend hours at that kitchen, I'm sure you'd be good at cooking."

"Why? Cuz I'm fat?"

I blow air out of my cheeks. "No, Tiff... Look, you're on that phone all day Tiff, it must hurt your eyes. Come spend some time with your old man for a sec, won't you?"

She doesn't say anything, she just keeps typing away. Angela walks through the door in her dental assistant scrubs. She sighs a big sigh and sets her purse down on the table and takes off her shoes. I scramble to the door and plant a big kiss on her cheek.

21

"Hi, honey," I say. "I'm so happy you're home." She looks at me funny. I reach for the flowers I bought her. "These are for you." I hold them out to her with a smile.

She looks at me funny some more. Well, first she looks at the flowers funny, then she looks at me funny again. "Did my mother die?" she asks and her face is suddenly really white.

"No, honey. These are just for you, just because."

"Oh… okay," she says. "I'll put them in some water."

She goes into the kitchen and gets out a vase. That look on her face has brought me down. I feel really stupid for going to any effort because I guess we aren't going to change and suddenly become happy like Max Adams and his perfect family and even Max Adams isn't happy so maybe nobody is happy and everyone is fucked and we're all going to die so why'd I even make dinner anyways? "Excuse me for a sec," I say. I head to the bathroom. I stare at myself in the mirror for so long that I start feeling really existential and weird like I don't exist and nothing is real.

I tell Tiff and Angela that I'm sick with the runs. I guzzle some Pepto-Bismol in front of them to bolster my lie. They eat dinner by themselves and don't say much. I suppose there isn't much to say. I go upstairs to rest.

A while later Ang enters the room. "What are you doing?" she says.

"Just resting," I say without even looking at her, still lying flat on the bed.

"Okay."

I sit up, propelled by some small stubborn hope. "Ang?"

"Yeah?"

"I... I'd really love to wash your hair in the bathtub. Like I used to when we were young. I can run you a bubble bath, with candles and—"

"Oh." She looks confused, uncomfortable, like I'm a stranger rather than her own husband. Like she doesn't even know me. Like she doesn't even want to. "Not tonight, Rex. I'm tired. And I just washed my hair this morning."

"Alright."

She walks into our bathroom and shuts the door. I lie down on our bed again like a beaten dog waiting to die.

Seven

I've been stalking Max Adams for over two weeks now and I don't know why. I still want revenge but I don't know what kind of revenge I want. I like watching him though, him and his perfect family. It's like looking into a dollhouse and watching plastic dolls move around like they've come to life. It's entertaining like a reality show. Spying on people makes me feel less alone, like my life is bigger than it is because it includes their lives too. Seeing Max Adams cry has also made me realize that happiness eludes us all because happiness is just a carrot society dangles in front of us that we can never reach.

Society runs on people's unhappiness. If people were happy, they wouldn't feel the need to buy the latest clothing and technology. That's why society tries to keep you very, very unhappy. The people on posters and magazines and TV are all better looking than you, and that makes you feel bad, and then they try to sell you things that they say will make you feel less bad, like makeup and exercise equipment. And I don't know how kids deal with life nowadays, with Instagram and TikTok and what have you. I watch Tiffany's fat finger scroll through pictures of these beautiful Photoshopped models all day and *ooh* and *ah* at their hair and lipstick and shit. Once, one of her stupid skinny friends was over, and they were on the couch scrolling through some famous girl's Instagram and Tiff's friend said "she's so pretty" and then Tiffany said "I know, I love her" and I remember my eyebrows creasing up while I was making a sandwich in the kitchen and I couldn't help but say something and I said, "you love her?"

Tiff looked at me like *why are you talking?* and her friend said, "yeah, she's so pretty". I spread some peanut butter on my bread and tried to keep quiet but then realized I couldn't because it was really irking me.

"Do you know this girl?" I asked.

Tiffany scoffed. "No, she's like the most famous model in the world, of course, we don't know her."

I started slicing some bananas to put on my sandwich. "But you love her... because she's pretty? Is that really a love-able quality?"

Tiffany rolled her eyes. "Ashley, let's go to my room, kay? My dad's being totally annoying right now." Her heavily made-up eyes shot me a death glare. I remember feeling so ashamed that that was my daughter.

The other night, Angela and I were lying in bed and I was staring up at the ceiling thinking about life and why we were so unhappy. I rolled over and said to Angela "are we happy?"

She didn't say anything for a long time but then she said "nobody's happy Rex, and the people who think they are, well, they're just running on false hope and caffeine."

"Doesn't that depress you, Ang?"

"Not really."

"Well, it depresses me. I think there's something wrong with me, Ang. It's like my head feels on fire sometimes that's how sad I am. It's like I can't believe the life I'm living, you know?"

She sighed and rolled away from me. "I don't want to talk about sad stuff."

That night, after Angela fell asleep, I snuck out and drove to Max Adams' house. It was very late, and all the lights were off. I just stood there by his back deck and looked at the moon and Lake Michigan and wished I was a different person. I wished I had never been born as myself and I wished Max Adams had never followed me into the forest that day and chosen me as the person to screw up for life. I hated Max Adams so much right then I could feel my fists curling up and I swear I almost broke into his house to wake him up from his perfect sleep beside his perfect wife by wrapping my hands around his muscly neck and slamming his beautiful head into the headboard a dozen times until he was dead and his blood was everywhere like my blood was on the snow that day.

I want to get inside Max Adams' house. I want to see where he sleeps and breathe in the same air as he does. I think maybe it would give me some ideas for revenge because none are really coming to me.

I try to think of ways I could get inside, but I guess there's really no way for me to get inside so I have to let it go, even though I really, really want to. I'm used to letting go of the things

I want. I've been doing it for quite some time. I think growing up is just the slow and painful letting go of all you've hoped for, I think that's really what it is. And it's a pain I don't wish on anybody, except Max Adams.

Eight

The sun looks really big in the sky like a very orange dodgeball. I'm driving my van again. It's noon. I see this boy on a bike waiting to cross the street. His bike is blue and he has long droopy hair. I swear it's like seeing Timothy's ghost and I almost cross two lanes of traffic I'm so spooked. Wow, does that boy look like Timothy. Except Timothy's bike was green and not blue but still, it really gives me the creeps and a horrible feeling in my stomach.

My friend Steve moved away when I was twelve and then I had no friends and I was feeling really alone in the world and whatnot and then a new family moved into Steve's old house and the parents had two sons. One son was named Doug. Doug was in his thirties but lived at home because he had Down syndrome. The other son was named Timothy and he was eight and he rode his green bike around all the time. One day we started talking about something, I don't even remember what, and then we started to talk a lot and I remember feeling really lame for having an eight-year-old friend but that's just what he was: a friend. It couldn't be avoided. He didn't have any friends either and he was always riding by my house on his bike and asking me what I was doing.

We used to ride bikes together after school. We were always going somewhere new, exploring some ravine or park. Timothy was such a nice person, it was like the niceness was oozing off of him and you couldn't help but think that he was going to do things right in his life, that he was gonna find some really nice girl one day and have really nice kids and tell them stories. And even though he was younger he was pretty cool. He had cool hair and his bike was cool too. I think I liked Timothy more than anyone else in the world. He was my best, best friend, a way better friend than Steve was.

Timothy always looked up to me. He always asked me about sex and girls like I had a clue. I always pretended I did just to impress him. Once, I remember we were riding bikes one day and he just started crying out of nowhere. I stopped my bike and asked him what was wrong and he said "why does my brother have to have Down syndrome? And why does my dad whip me with his belt? And why is my mom so sad all the time?" I remember thinking it was probably the saddest stuff I'd ever heard. I hugged Timothy tight and told him things would get better even though I didn't really believe that at all.

I was so happy that Timmy lived next door to me and that I got to be his friend because Timmy had a pretty bad life. I mean, our families were both on the poor side but his family was poorer and their house looked awful poor. It was always dark inside his house and his Down syndrome brother was always screaming about something and his mother reminded me of a vacant building like if you looked through her windows there'd be nothing there, no furniture or lamps or anything, and his dad was unemployed and grumbly and he would sit on the couch from morning to night and stare at the TV with a beer in his hand and his beer gut all jiggly. Tim's dad was a shell, and not the pretty kind you press to your ear to hear the ocean. If you pressed your ear to Timmy's dad, I doubt you'd even hear a heartbeat.

Timothy didn't like to be in his house because there was always a lot of yelling or a lot of quiet and no in between, so he would always be riding his bike around. I think he didn't get enough to eat at his house and I think that was why he was always so skinny and that made me really sad. I always had good food at my house on account of being Italian so I would invite him over a lot for dinner and he would eat so much spaghetti and my mother loved him like a son of her own and she was glad that he liked her cooking so much.

Even though his life was pretty shitty, Timmy was usually smiling and was almost never sad. He loved nature and he was always wowing at everything like different flowers and bugs. He knew so much about so much because he was always reading the encyclopedia like it was as easy as reading a comic book. I remember the first day we invited Timmy on a Sunday drive. You would have thought he was going to Disney World or something he was so excited. He wore his best shirt which was a light blue button down and it made his eyes look so blue.

That day we went to a park out of town and it was a gorgeous day with the sky as blue as Timmy's shirt and eyes and Timmy was so happy it was like he was going to burst. He kept talking and talking the whole car ride and he told us all about different animals and different plants and all kinds of things and my mom was smiling so much as Timothy talked and gesticulated like crazy with his eyes all electric and happy. When we got to the park, we spread out a picnic blanket and took out sandwiches from the picnic basket and I remember some ants came around and I started killing them and then Timothy said "no, no don't kill them!" and then he started scooping them up in his hand and a few bit him but he still didn't kill them and he watched them crawl around his hand and his arm and he started telling us all these wild facts about ants that blew my mind and then I felt bad for ever killing any.

After lunch, I went back to the car and got out a brand-new kite that I had bought for Timmy with my paper route money. It had a shark's face on it. I bought it for Timmy because sharks were his favorite animal. He smiled so big when he saw it and he hugged me with his gangly arms and he told me he'd never flown a kite before. I couldn't believe it so then I taught him to fly the kite and he was so happy when he got the hang of it. He kept running through the grass with the kite and he was so excited about it that it even made my sister smile and my sister was usually all moody and sexy and ultra-cool and she never had time for Timothy and me because we were just "little pervs" to her that stared at her friends' asses but even she got up and started running beside us like she was a little girl. The three of us ran and ran and I tried to keep up but I couldn't because

of my limp but I was so happy seeing Timothy and my sister
running around and jumping around and my sister doing cart-
wheels once in a while and laughing a whole lot and for once
she wasn't worried about her hair or nails or anything and then I
was suddenly really happy that Timothy was a little kid because
he was still filled with a lot of wonder and he reminded me
that there was still a lot of happiness and magic in the world.

"That was the best day of my life," Timothy said on the
car ride home. He was holding on to his shark kite tight like
it might fly away even though it couldn't because it was all
folded up in his lap and we were inside the car. My parents and
my sister and I were all speechless because it was crazy that a
Sunday drive could be the best day of someone's life and I think
it made us all realize that his life must be pretty bad, even worse
than we thought, and from then on we invited him on every
Sunday drive and after every Sunday drive he would say it was
the new best day of his life and I'm really glad that the best days
of Timothy's life were with me and I think the best days of my
life were with Timothy too and it's funny when you're young
you don't ever think that Sunday drives will wind up being the
best days of your life.

I remember once Max Adams and his lackeys teased me
at the ice cream store for being friends with Timothy because
he was a little kid. They called him "my little butt buddy". I'm
ashamed to admit it, but I remember something changed in me
that day and I was really embarrassed about being Timothy's
friend. I would still spend time with him but I never wanted

to leave the neighborhood anymore or go on Sunday drives cuz I didn't want anybody to see us together and in the back of my mind I was always thinking "why am I hanging out with a little kid?" I have to stop thinking about Timothy now because it makes me too sad.

Nine

Since I saw that boy that looked like Timothy on that blue bike, I keep dreaming of Timothy riding around on his green bike and I really hope that he's in a better place than here because I think living here on earth is just awful. I hate most things about being alive. I hate watching everyone stare down at their cell phones all day. I hate watching people in shopping malls, buying things they don't need. I hate how almost nobody smiles at strangers. I hate rich people like Max Adams and his family. I hate capitalism. I hate brushing my teeth. I hate how my wife and I watch TV every night and wait to die.

What I dream about most are Timothy's shoes. Timothy's shoes scare me more than any nightmare about a witch or a murderer ever could. I'm sorry, Timothy. I'm so sorry I could start crying right now, but I can't because I'm with my family and we're sitting in the living room and I'm the man of the house and if a man cries he's a sissy so men just have to bottle up their feelings until they're found in their office or bedroom with a gunshot in the head or a noose around their neck and maybe if we just had someone to talk to or a shoulder to cry on we wouldn't have had to do that.

God, I can't stand watching Tiffany on that phone. Who the hell is she talking to anyway? "Who are you talking to on that phone?" I ask her. She looks up at me. It's a strange thing to see her face because she's usually staring down at that goddamned phone. Her face is like two faces smooshed together.

"Nobody," she says.

I rub my temples. Angela's staring at the TV, her hand in the popcorn dish, sitting amongst pillows donning needlepoint quotes about hope and adventure, as if placed there to mock us. It's like she's not even here. Her eyes are empty. I know she checked out of this life a long time ago. She's just waiting for some kind of cancer to kick in and take her away.

"Why do you think we're alive?" Timothy asked me once. We were lying on a blanket in my backyard looking at the stars.

I shrugged. I was fifteen at the time. It was only a few weeks before Max Adams would change my life forever. My head was crystal clear and I was nothing but normal. "To try and score chicks," I said.

Timothy laughed. He was eleven by then, and still really lanky, with long limbs and long, long hair. "I'm serious, Rex."

"Then I don't know."

Timothy folded his arms behind his head. I remember the stars reflected in his eyes. "What do you want to be when you're older?"

"I don't know. I'll probably end up selling insurance or something."

"Why do you say that?"

"Cuz that's what my dad does. And I don't have the looks to be famous, or the grades to be a successful businessman or anything like that. Maybe I'll be a mailman... or a fry cook."

"But what do you really want to be?"

"Seen." The word tumbled from my mouth before I even had the chance to think about it.

"What do you mean?"

I shrugged. "I don't know, it's stupid."

"It's not stupid."

I sighed. "Well, I guess I don't really care about what I'm going to do for a living. I just feel so invisible all the time. I just want to stop feeling invisible. I live my life in the shadows. It's pathetic, Tim. I need to grow a pair. I need to stand up to Max Adams and all those other assholes, not let them push us around anymore. And I wish I didn't have my limp, and I wish I was good-looking like my sister. I wish my dad wasn't ashamed of me."

Timmy propped himself up on his skinny little elbows and looked at me. "You're not invisible, Rex. Not to me."

We were quiet for a while, gazing up at a white sliver of moon. I turned my head a little because I didn't want Timmy to see the tears in my eyes. "Well thanks, Tim. What do you wanna be when you grow up?"

"Well, I always thought I'd be a scientist, but my biggest dream is to go to space one day. So I've decided I'm gonna be an astronaut."

That seemed awful far out to me. "What do you mean *decided*? What if you don't get to be?"

"Well, then I'll be happy doing whatever I'm doing. As long as I can always keep my telescope and keep looking at the stars, I'll be happy. I just need to get out of the house. What do you say we run away somewhere?"

"And where would we go?"

A sadness passed over Timothy's starlit face. "Somewhere my dad can't find me."

That tied a knot in my stomach. "You should kill him," I whispered. "You could poison him, or push him down the stairs."

"But I love him."

"What the fuck do you mean?"

"I mean, my dad's a bad man in a lot of ways but he's a good man in a lot of ways, too. It's hard to explain. Like the time he taught me to play poker. He was so happy that night. He let me sip his beer and we laughed our heads off about stupid stuff. That was one of my favorite times."

There was rage inside me. "He beats you!"

"Yeah, I know. And his daddy beat him. And you know what, Rex? I'm glad he beats me. If he has to beat someone, I'm glad it's me because it means he doesn't lay a hand on Doug. At least I have a chance of getting out of that house one day. Doug will never go anywhere. So I'll take all the beatings I can for him, and if you were my brother, I'd take them for you too. When my dad takes out his belt, it's almost comforting, because I'd like to think he's wearing himself out, getting it out of his system, and when it comes time for me to leave for astronaut school, he'll be a shriveled up old man with no fight left in him, and he'll leave Doug and my mom the hell alone."

I glared at him. "You're fucked up, Timmy! God, I'd kill your dad if I could. And I'd kill Max Adams and all his stupid friends. I'd blow them all up like fireworks."

Timothy clucked his tongue. He looked up at the sky like he was the wisest person in the world. "I like to think of anger like one big game of hot potato," he said. "It's like, everybody's got this hot potato of rage boiling inside them and it's burning them real bad so they pass it on to the next person and then that person passes it to the next person, and so on and it never ends and then we all die. And I can't imagine ever beating somebody up or being mean to somebody, so those people, the people like my dad and the bullies at school must have the hottest potatoes of all. I can't even imagine how burning hot their potatoes are."

I shook my head. I was still so mad thinking of Timmy's dad beating on him. "You'll see one day when you get a little older. Then you'll see the truth of things," I said.

Timothy just kept staring at the sky.

Ten

I'm driving to the Adams' suburb and as I drive, I keep thinking the same thought and the thought is this: My whole life, I've been waiting for something. Anything. Just something to happen. All of my days look the same. I never go anywhere new or interesting. We never have the money to go on vacation. I've never been out of the U.S. I don't have any friends. I have a fat, sexless wife and a second mortgage. I've always wanted to be saved by something.

After that day out in the forest, I tried really hard to get better. After the initial shock of it all, I had to get on with things. I poured my time into Angela and trying to be a good brother and son. I saved up my money one Christmas and bought my sister a new sewing machine she'd wanted for a long time. I think seeing her open that sewing machine will always be one of my favorite memories.

I've been a pretty good guy my whole life. I've never cheated on my wife or stolen anything. It's almost like I thought I'd be rewarded someday. Like some Big Miraculous Change would happen. Like I'd win the lottery or suddenly become really good-looking. But nothing happened, not until I saw Max Adams again.

I think I need to do something big. I think I need to kill Max Adams. I think Max Adams coming back into my life is the Big Miraculous Change that I've been waiting for. Max Adams has caused so much suffering. Max Adams wasn't a normal high school bully. He was something so much worse. There was something feral in his eyes, something that wanted to do some real damage.

He used to stalk me like his prey, wait for me after school, leaning up against my locker with that crooked evil grin on his face. *Where ya going, Gimpy?* I remember how he'd trip me when I walked by, watch me fall to the floor, my books scatter on the linoleum. I remember how he'd kick me in the ribs when no one was around, so hard it would knock the wind out of me. I remember when he once poured milk down my backpack and wrecked all of my books. I remember how he and his friends crowded around me and Timmy one day when we were walking down the street. I remember the flash of Max Adams' knife. He held it up to Timmy's fluttering neck. I swear my heart almost gave out. "I own you, butt fucks," he said and his friends all laughed. "I tell you where to go and what to do. I own you." Before he turned to leave, he cut Timmy's neck, not a deep cut, but a cut deep enough to leave a scar and I just stood there, scared half to death. But I'm not scared anymore. Now I'm the one in control, the one holding that figurative knife. I walk up to Max Adams' house and smile Max Adams' evil half-smile. *I own you, Max Adams, you motherfucker. I own you.*

I pull into the Adams' suburb and park in my around-the-block spot. I get out of the car and walk through the forest to Max Adams' house. So yeah, I really want to kill Max Adams. I think I really, really do. But I don't want to go to prison. I'd have to make his death look like an accident. I think pushing him down the stairs when he's home alone is a good idea but I don't know how to get into his house and I don't think pushing him down the stairs would kill him. He has too many muscles. Maybe I could electrocute him somehow, like do something to his toaster or something but again I don't know how to get into his house. Fuck. I kick a rock down the street with my good leg. I wish I could just go up to Max Adams and start strangling him and watch all the light fade from his eyes. I want him to know it was me who killed him. I want me to be the last thing he ever sees.

Someone is screaming. A little girl's scream. Right here in the forest. I crouch down low behind a fallen tree trunk. I see Max Adams fly out the side door and into the forest. I travel by trees to get a closer look, hiding behind ones with wide enough trunks. I see Max Adams has come across his daughter. She's sitting atop a pile of autumn leaves beside her small treehouse, clutching her leg as though it's been hurt. I reach a large tree about fifteen feet away from them and stay put.

"What happened, Pumpkin?" I hear Max Adams say.

"I was climbing up to the tree house," his daughter says. "And one of the ladder rungs broke and I cut myself. Do I need stitches, daddy?"

"No Pumpkin. I think a little Neosporin will do the trick." I steal a glance at them from behind the tree. Max Adams stands up, takes his daughter's hands and helps her to her feet. "I'm so glad you're okay, Liv. When I heard you screaming it scared me half to death."

"I'm fine, daddy. I'm sorry I scared you. My leg doesn't hurt that bad but I think I'll need some ice cream to fully heal."

He laughs. "Okay."

"Can I have a piggyback ride?" she asks, their backs now to me.

"Of course, Pumpkin." She hops onto his back. He spins around a few times and her hair goes flying behind her and then wraps around her neck like a scarf. She giggles.

"Daddy, do you love me more than Thomas?" she asks.

"No, Pumpkin. I love you and Thomas equally. I love you and Thomas as much as anyone can possibly love anybody."

"I think you're kidding yourself, Daddy. I think you love me more and I know that mommy is the best mommy in the world and all, but you're my favorite, Daddy," she says.

Max begins walking back toward the house, holding onto his daughter by her little pink running shoes, her arms fastened around his neck. "If I tell you something, you have to promise me you'll never ever tell Thomas or mommy or anyone else. Do you promise, Olivia?"

"Yes, I promise."

They're nearly out of earshot now, their voices fading into the forest. Faintly, as though in a whisper, I hear Max's secret:

"You're my favorite too."

Eleven

There must be some really good stuff in my heart because for a second when I'm watching Max and his daughter together, I almost want to forget all about killing him but that's crazy. *This is for Timothy*, I think to myself, *you need to kill Max Adams for Timothy's sake. Max Adams deserves a thousand deaths for what he's done.*

I'm still feeling a little sad about the prospect of leaving Max's kids without a father, but then I tell myself that maybe Max Adams has done what he did to me to other people. Maybe he's still doing it. I need to shield the world from his wrath. It feels like I finally have a calling. Like I finally belong to something bigger than myself.

I sit in my car in Max's suburb. It's raining and I watch raindrops race down the windshield. I force myself to remember that day out in the forest. I haven't let myself relive it in over a decade because it makes me start crying and it makes me feel like I don't belong in my skin, like I want to jump out of my skin and then burn it and then watch my skin burning, but I want to get angry again. I sit there with my head against the headrest and my eyes closed with nothing but the sound of the driving rain and I make myself remember everything.

So I was in the forest. And I was feeling happy and Christmassy. And then that twig broke, and Max Adams was chasing after me—*you can't run, Gimpy, not with that limp, you can't run away*—and then he was right behind me. He grabbed my arms, his hands like tourniquets, and put them behind my back. I tried to fight back but he was so strong and tall. He got on top of me and straddled my legs. He let go of my arms for a second and I tried to hit him but I couldn't reach him. "Stop thrashing around or I'll knock you out," he said.

I didn't understand what he wanted with me until he pulled down my jeans. I tried to buck him off me like a bull, and that's when I felt a sharp pain in my head and that's when I passed out. He had hit me with a rock. I came to a few minutes later and I felt the worst pain in my ass. Max Adams was raping me. I screamed and he hit me with the rock again and everything went black. I came to again right when he was zipping up his pants. I was still lying on the ground and I was crying hard now and my bare legs were freezing in the snow. I looked beside me and I could see blood on the snow from him raping me and blood on the snow from him hitting my head with that rock. I looked up at him through teary eyes and he cast his eyes down. I started screaming, wanting someone to catch him. He whipped out his glittering knife and pointed it at me. "You tell anyone about this, Gimpy, and I'll kill your whole family." I stopped screaming.

I remember I just laid there bawling for a while after he was gone and it was getting dark and I thought "I'm gonna be late for dinner" and I couldn't believe that I could have a thought like that after what had just happened and I couldn't believe that life just went on after something like that. I pulled my pants up and my ass and head hurt something terrible. I pushed myself up off the bloody snow and I started to limp out of the forest and back home. Sometimes little drops of blood plopped onto the snow as I walked. I remember I had tears in my eyes still so all the Christmas lights in my neighborhood were foggy. I was cold and in a lot of pain. I felt dirty and disgusting and worse than I'd ever felt and Max Adams raping me was worse than him beating me up a thousand times and I had never felt less like myself ever and it was like I didn't even know who I was or where I was or why I had been born at all.

I saw Timothy riding down the street on his green bicycle. "Hey pal," he said as if nothing was wrong. I remember I got so mad at him then. It was like there was a whole holocaust inside me. I had thought that Max Adams raped me because he knew I couldn't run away because of my limp, but when I saw Timmy it occurred to me that maybe Max Adams raped me because he thought I was a secret homo too because I was always hanging around Timmy and Max Adams and his friends were always calling him "my little butt buddy". "What are you all sour about?" Timothy asked when I didn't say hi back.

I remember my teeth clenching up. "Get away from me, faggot!"

Timothy staggered backward. "Rex..."

"I never want to see you again!" I was crying and my fists were all balled up.

45

I'm crying and shaking now in the car seat as I think about it and it's like I'm there again, looking into Timothy's big blue eyes as they fill with tears and hurt. "Rex... I don't understand... you're my best friend."

"Well, you're not mine!" I remember my spit flying out at him. "I only hung out with you because I felt bad for you. You're just an annoying little kid to me. That's all you ever were and I have no time for you anymore. You ruined my life. I... I hate you!"

Timothy got back on his bike and pedaled away crying and I stood there on the curb crying and then I went inside my house for dinner and I barely ate a thing and all I kept thinking was *I have to go say sorry to Timmy* because I loved him even more than I hated Max Adams and I was thinking about him and his feelings even more than I was thinking about how I'd just been raped and I thought about Tim's daddy beating on him and what a good kid he was and how his brother had Down syndrome and how he hadn't a single friend but me and I felt just rotten.

I excused myself from dinner and ran up to my room and my ass and head were still throbbing and stinging. Timothy's bedroom window faced mine and when we wanted to talk to each other we would hold up a piece of paper to the window that said what we wanted to say. I was gonna hold up a piece of paper that said how sorry I was and then hopefully Timmy would forgive me. I always saw Timmy at his desk doing his homework but when I got to the window, he wasn't there but I could see his shoes and I thought *why are his shoes dangling in the air?* and then I saw that his shoes were attached to his legs.

46

I cried out and I ran down the stairs and out into the snow and I remember it was snowing and the snow was flurrying out in front of me and I ran to Timothy's house and I knocked so hard that I almost knocked the door down and his mother answered and I pushed right past her and ran up the stairs and then there was Timmy, strung up from his bedroom ceiling with his hair falling like a curtain over his eyes and a noose around his broken neck.

I started screaming and his mother came up and she started screaming and I jumped on top of Timmy's bed, on top of his bedspread filled with planets and stars and threadbare holes, and I got him down from the noose and I put him down on the bed and I shook his shoulders and his mother ran out of the room screaming and crying down the hall to the phone and called an ambulance. I sat over Timmy and I checked his pulse and there was no pulse and then I knew he was dead and that nothing could bring him back and I thought that maybe I should hang myself from that noose strung up from the ceiling too and I couldn't believe that he was alive and riding his green bike just a few hours ago and now he was dead forever.

I started howling and crying and shaking and I moved Timmy's long hair back and I saw his dead face and it was like I was in hell. I looked out the window at the stars and I saw Timothy's telescope at the window and I thought about how he'd never be an astronaut and how he'd never see the stars again. It was like every star was his friend and he knew so many of their names and now he'd never see them again and I was the best friend Timothy ever had and I was horrible to him and now he's dead.

Timmy looked so long and skinny in his coffin. I never cried at his funeral. Not a tear. I wanted to cry but I couldn't, maybe because crying didn't seem like enough. To cry seemed too insignificant a gesture. I wanted to give him my skin. I wanted to fold it up and place it in his casket so a part of me would be rotting there with him. I thought about how Vincent van Gogh cut his ear off for some girl and how, if I could ever cut my ear off for anybody, it would be for Timmy.

I didn't say anything at his funeral because I was still shaken up and filled with so much hate and hurt and to this day it's one of my biggest regrets because no one said anything about Timmy except for his mother who said that he was a "good boy". I remember Timmy's brother was screeching like a half-runover animal, and that embarrassed his dad a lot because his parents never really brought Doug out of the house and everyone was staring at him. I wish I had stood at that podium and said that Timmy was the best friend any guy could ever hope to have, and I didn't give a fuck what kids said about him being my little butt buddy and I didn't care if he was still a little kid because he was better than anyone else in the world and I would miss riding bikes with him and seeing him go down the street on his green bike.

After Timmy hung himself, I was so mad at Max Adams that I felt like screaming all day long and I couldn't believe that Timmy died thinking that I hated him. He died thinking that nobody loved him at all I'm sure. My mom let me stay home from school for two whole weeks after Timmy died, which was just about the nicest thing anyone's ever done for me. For those two weeks, I lay in my bed staring at the walls and thinking that I should have died instead of Timmy and thinking that Max Adams should die and I thought that if Max Adams raped me again, I would probably kill myself too.

Life was so lonely without Timmy. My sister brought me to the park a few days after he died and that was nice of her. She just sat with me as we stared up at the sky. She saw a cloud that looked like a heart and I saw a cloud that looked like a dolphin. My sister wasn't full of bullshit like most people and she wasn't afraid of silence. She didn't run her mouth for no reason and I liked just sitting with her and watching the clouds but I missed Timmy something terrible. It was like my heart had been torn into a million fleshy pieces and then I pictured my heart torn into a million fleshy pieces and all the blood and disgustingness of that and it reminded me of Max Adams raping me and the blood it left behind and a really unsettling thought popped into my head and the thought was that if I went back to that exact spot in the forest my blood would still be there under a new layer of snow.

I was scared shitless to go back to school and see Max Adams and I never walked through the forest again but by some miracle, Max Adams must have moved schools or his parents must have moved towns or something because I never saw him again. It was surprising the way life just went on after

Timmy died. I started making myself really busy so I didn't have to think about Timmy or Max Adams and I joined the science club because I liked science and I even made some friends but none as good as Timmy. And then Angela moved in and I fixated on her and then I married her and then we had Tiffany and now I'm here.

But, even after all these years, every time I'm falling asleep and I'm in that weird between sleep and awake phase where your body jolts I'm always right back in that forest and it's like I can almost smell Max Adams, and how he smelled like sweat and desperation and I can almost feel the pain in my ass and head and then I see Timmy's shoes suspended in the air through his window.

Twelve

I'm mad and sad all the next day too because those memories won't stop playing in my head. It's Sunday morning and Tiffany's in her pajamas lying on the couch staring at her phone. It's such a beautiful day and I really want to get out of my bad mood so I say to Tiffany "hey, kiddo, when I was young my parents used to take me on Sunday drives and we would always go someplace really beautiful and I think you and me should do that today, what do you say kiddo?"

She doesn't look up from her phone. "I'm busy, dad."

I scratch the back of my neck. "I should get you a t-shirt, Tiff. A t-shirt that says 'I'm busy'." I say it with a laugh but inside I'm still angry. I'm angry that Tiffany would waste a beautiful day like this being on her phone and I'm angry that she never wants to spend any time with me and I'm angry that she's fat and uninteresting and an idiot. She doesn't even laugh or snort or acknowledge what I said.

My blood starts boiling. "Tiffany, your father is talking to you." She looks up for a sec and makes a face at me and then looks back down at her phone. "Tiffany, can't you see that I just want to spend time with you!" I scream. I'd never screamed at her before and she looks surprised. I stand up. I'm so mad I'm shaking. I grab the phone out of her hand and throw it down on the ground. I stomp all over it until it's only glass and wires on the carpet. God, I'm glad Angela's not home because she'd be awful mad at me if she'd seen this.

The way Tiff screamed you'd think I'd killed her only child if she'd had one. She storms upstairs to her room but I'm not done. I follow her upstairs. I push my way into her room even though she's trying to lock the door on me. I go over to her desk and get her laptop and take it to my room. She jumps on top of my back. God, she's fat. I somehow manage to get her off and I quickly open the safe in the closet and I lock the laptop inside. She sits on my bed and cries and thrashes her arms around and screams: "I hate you, I hate you!"

I stand up over her. I'm panting hard because that was very stressful and tiring and I say "no more phone, no more computer, not until you figure out how to be a real goddamn person". I leave her there crying and screaming and flopping around like a very fat fish out of water.

I decide to go to Max Adams' house to look for ideas of how to kill him. I'm so angry at Tiff and at Max Adams that if I saw Max Adams outside getting the mail or something, I may have no control and just run him over but then it would be over too quickly and I'd have to go back to my normal, purposeless life of waiting to die. When I get there, Max Adams isn't out getting the mail. Both cars are gone and that's great because now I can do some real snooping. I walk up to the house and look through the windows at the shiny chandeliers and fancy furniture and try really hard to figure out a way to get in the house but I can't come up with anything logical. I couldn't pretend to be an old friend or something because his whole family had seen me on their camping misadventure and knew that Max Adams was afraid of me. I could wear a fake nose or beard or something but I don't think I could pull that off and besides, there's no possible way I can hide my limp, unless I show up in a wheelchair.

Maybe I could wait one night for Max Adams to go outside again like that one time he cried and looked out over Lake Michigan and then drown him in Lake Michigan but if I'm being serious, I know that Max Adams is much stronger than me and that he would probably end up being the one drowning me.

I see a little squirrel run past me and into the forest and I think that squirrel was sent from God above because I got this idea that hit me like a bolt of lightning. I remembered how Max ran into the forest when he heard his little blonde daughter screaming. I could dig a hole, set some sort of booby trap near the tree house, with knives at the bottom that would impale him, and then I could hide behind a tree in direct line of the hole and then I could scream and keep screaming and then Max Adams would come running toward me and fall into the hole and then I could look in the hole and see him impaled with knives throughout his body.

Wow, do I like that idea. I got the idea from the Punji stick trap, which was used in the Vietnam War. It consisted of digging a hole and shoving sharpened bamboo sticks into the bottom of it. Then, the hole was camouflaged by leaves, just waiting for some unlucky soldier to walk upon it. The Punji stick trap usually just injured soldiers, but if I swapped out bamboo sticks for steaks knives, and dug a hole deep enough for gravity to do some real damage, I can't see it being anything but lethal. I would have to work all through the night to dig the hole and it would have to be a weekend so Max Adams would be home. I'd need to make sure that his wife wasn't there so she didn't run out instead of Max Adams when I screamed.

I walk back to my car. I'm shaky and excited because it all seems real now and I'm actually going to kill Max Adams, holy shit. Now, I have to be very careful not to get caught. When Max Adams is dead, the police will ask his wife if she knows anyone who would have wanted him dead, and if she knows anything about his evil past, a lot of people might come to mind but I don't think she knows a thing because who would be with a man like that if she did? But maybe she'll think of me and how I followed them to that campsite. Maybe she remembers my name. Or maybe she doesn't. It's a risk I'm willing to take. I'd take just about any risk to see Max Adams all bloody and dead at the bottom of a hole.

So, I need to buy a bunch of knives but I can't risk buying them in a regular store like Walmart. The police would dig up purchase records of who had bought those specific knives and, even if I paid in cash so the store had no record of me, and wore a big coat and a hat and sunglasses, Max Adams' family could still recognize me on the store's security footage thanks to my limp. I think my safest bet is to buy some knives from different thrift stores way out of town.

When I have that thought about security footage the blood drains from my face. The Adams could very well have surveillance cameras set up outside their house. I've been stalking them for a while now and as soon as Max Adams is killed, they'll look at the footage and see me. I quickly search around the outside of their house for security cameras but I don't find any. When I get home, I Google what percentage of houses have surveillance cameras and a study says only about eighteen percent, which gives me some relief but then I start chewing my lip until it's raw because eighteen percent is still a lot of percent and am I sure that I checked his house for cameras well enough?

I go back another day when both cars are gone and look around for cameras again and still don't find any but I'm still chewing my lip a lot because the neighbors could have security cameras and maybe the police would ask them for the footage after Max Adams is dead and maybe their cameras have captured me limping around the Adams' house.

It's a terrifying venture, the whole thing, but worth it, I think. I mean, what else am I living for anyway? If I go to prison for the rest of my days, at least I'd die knowing that I'd done something with my life. Besides, it's not like Tiff or Angela would miss me.

Thirteen

S o I've bought a dozen different steak knives from several
different thrift stores out of town and, whenever I'm not in
my van, I'm out in the woods next to Max Adams' house gathering
sticks. It's a really scary thing to do, because twice now, I've had
to dodge behind a tree and stay there for a good hour because
Max Adams' two kids have been out in the forest playing tag or
hide and seek and came very close to seeing me.

I've burned the bottom of my shoes so they don't leave Nike
imprints anymore and I make sure I wear gloves so there's no
chance of fingerprints. I collect a bunch of twigs, and I find more
sticks, slightly longer, fatter ones than twigs and it takes forever
but I tie the slightly fatter, longer sticks together with some
friendship bracelet string until I have something about six feet
by three feet that resembles a rectangular pretzel like the little
Snyder's ones you can buy in the bag with all the little squares
in them like apartment building windows and then I fill all the
squares with the twigs and glue them in place with a glue stick.
When I'm all done I hide the covering under a bunch of leaves.

Tomorrow's the day. A Saturday. I had to skip a week
because Max Adams' wife was home for the weekend, but I've

been hanging around their deck every day since I decided to kill Max Adams while they drink their disgusting green juices and talk about rich people things and sure enough, his wife has a hair appointment on Saturday at four thirty.

I have the day off but I told Tiff and Angela that I'd be gone for the night because I was taking a delivery driver friend's shift because his wife was giving birth in the hospital. If Tiff or Angela knew me at all they would know that I don't have any friends but they don't really know me because they don't really care so Angela just grumbles a goodbye from her place on the couch watching TV and Tiff says nothing and stares at the TV instead of her phone because I took it away and she still hates me for it.

I grab a shovel from the garage and put it in the back of the car. I wrap up all the knives in a thrifted sheet. I pack a thrifted rope ladder so I can get out of the hole once I dig it. I drive to Max Adams' house. I park even further down the street than usual just to be safe. I get out of my car and creep into the forest with my shovel and rope ladder. I head to the tree house, then I walk about twenty feet to the side of the tree house to dig the hole so one of Max Adams' kids doesn't accidentally fall in if they went to the tree house the next morning or something. God, what if one of his kids accidentally falls in?

I want to kill Max Adams so badly that I tell myself that there is zero chance that Max Adams' kids would be out playing twenty feet to the side of the tree house. I decide that I will dig the hole an extra twenty feet to the side of the treehouse just to be safe. I convince myself that there is absolutely no reason why Max Adams' kids would go forty feet to the side of the tree house, but then I realize that Max Adams probably wouldn't hear me screaming tomorrow if I'm forty feet to the side of the tree house. I start panicking. I shut my eyes tight and finally decide that I should dig the hole thirty feet to the side of the tree house and then scream with all my might.

I start to dig in a soft, mossy part of the forest floor with a nervousness in my stomach. I keep worrying about finding one of his kids' bodies impaled in the hole tomorrow but I keep telling myself that that's preposterous until I actually start to believe it (it's funny the things you will believe when you're desperate to believe them) and then I feel better about things and excited that Max Adams is going to die tomorrow. The hole is very deep. It took me many hours to dig and made it all the more obvious that I'm very, very out of shape because I'm crazy winded and my arms feel like noodles. I go back to my car and take the knives over to the hole. I collect twelve long sticks and sharpen them at the bottoms with one of the steak knives. I attach each of the twelve knives to each of the twelve sticks with twine I'd thrifted, wrapping the twine around and around the knife handles many times before tying it off. Then I push the sticks deep into the soil up past the knife handles, so the sharp knife tips only stick out a little over halfway. I pack dirt tightly around them, so they're standing sturdy enough to pierce flesh and not topple over when Max Adams falls on them. I crawl out of the hole and put my hands on my hips and look long and hard at the trap and think long and hard about if I really want to kill Max Adams or not and the answer is still yes. The knives look so ominous like out of a horror movie.

I go back to the tree that contains the stick covering I'd made and I carry over the covering. I put the covering on top of the hole and then I carry a bunch of autumn leaves over to the covering to conceal it. It's done. I take the shovel and ladder and sheet back to the car. I drive away knowing that Max Adams will be dead tomorrow. I turn the radio up. It's some shitty pop song I don't know but I crank it up anyways. I feel very alive. I drive about thirty minutes out of town to dispose of the shovel and ladder and sheet. I throw the shovel in a dumpster down some alley and then I throw the sheet in another dumpster and the ladder in another dumpster. Then I go to a Walmart, park my car and sleep in the parking lot.

Fourteen

I wake up in my car seat with a very sore neck. I had the craziest dream about a booby trap I'd made to kill Max Adams and then I realize that it wasn't a dream and that it's real life and I'm actually going to kill Max Adams and I can't breathe for a second. Did I want to kill Max Adams? I start having a lot of thoughts. I mean, yes, he's done unspeakable things, but that was a lifetime ago. Max may very well be a decent person now. But can a person who holds someone down in the snow, who bashes their head with a rock and cuts their asshole up raping them ever be a good person? Does a person like that deserve to go on with their rich little life with their rich little job in their rich little house with their rich little family? Does a person like that deserve fancy cars and fancy haircuts and a wife with the pert, perfect ass of a twenty-year-old?

I start getting really mad again and I'm glad for it. I felt too soft a minute ago. Of course, Max Adams deserves to die.

The thing that makes me really happy about this whole killing Max Adams business is that handsome, rich guys like Max Adams think nothing bad is ever going to happen to them. It's like they feel invincible I think, like the kings of the world.

And they never think that the ugly quiet kid with the limp that they messed with in school will come back to kill them one day. They never see it coming. That's the real beauty in all of this.

Wow, am I fired up now! I drive to McDonald's for breakfast. I order two coffees and they get me extra fired up. I find a heavy metal station on the radio and thrash my head around to the music. I feel like a teenager driving to a party, but when I get to Max Adams' suburb my stomach lurches and the caffeine suddenly makes me really nervous instead of fired up and I pray that I won't find one of his kids' bodies in the hole.

I park in my usual spot. I sneak into the forest. It's early, way earlier than 4:30 p.m., but I want to just sit in anticipation for a while. Once Max Adams is dead, this will all be over and, apart from living in constant dread of the police knocking on my door, everything will go back to being boring. I have to prolong the happening. I decide to walk up to Max Adams' house for a little spying session. I need to see Max Adams alive, one last time.

I go to look through the window like usual but there's a woman walking her dog on the sidewalk who might see me, so I stay at the forest's edge, get out a pair of binoculars from my backpack and focus them on the side window. I can see Max Adams and his wife and kids in their sparkly kitchen making pancakes. They all look so happy. The little girl's ponytail is swinging and she keeps looking at Max like he's just the greatest thing, and the wife looks so pretty and perfect in her silk housecoat with her face all bare and moisturized. The wife flips a pancake high up into the air and almost doesn't catch it but then she does catch it and the son laughs. It makes me sad looking at them because it reminds me of how good things used to be with Tiffany when she was little, back when she used to love me.

As I'm watching them, I keep thinking that maybe I don't want to kill Max and I hate myself for being such a softie sucker but the thought won't leave me alone. It's irritating, like a bee buzzing around my head.

I don't want to kill Max. Not anymore. Yes, Max Adams has done unspeakable things to me, and yes, he's pretty much the reason Timothy is dead, but did I really want to become a murderer? Did I really want to leave Max's kids without a father, gift them a fucked-up childhood like mine? And the thing I've just realized now, the thing I think I was too clouded by anger to see, is that I don't think Timothy would have wanted any of this. I don't think he would have even had the time to bother with thoughts of revenge. He would have been too busy looking at the stars.

I run back to my Subaru all panicked to grab my shovel so I can fill in the hole and forget all about this, but then I remember that I'd gotten rid of it the night before. Holy hell. I get in my car, start the engine. I'd have to buy a new shovel. I don't have to worry about purchase records anymore, because I'm going to undo everything. All the knives would be buried. This entire horrible mistake would be buried.

I drive to Walmart, buy a shovel, get back in the car. I drive as fast as I can back to the Adams' suburb. When I'm back in the forest with my new shovel, I check the trap again with my heart beating like crazy. No one's fallen in it, thank god.

I hear footsteps. Max's two kids are in the forest. I dodge behind big tree. I hear a voice. It's the son's—Thomas, that's his name, I remember now. He's counting, leaning up against a tree about twenty feet from mine. "…Forty-seven, forty-eight, forty-nine, fifty. Ready or not, here I come!" Thomas takes off running, his blue scarf flapping in the wind. He's running right toward the hole. My heart leaps up into my throat. I want to cry out, want to tell him to stop, that—

The flash of Olivia's blonde ponytail whips past me. She runs toward the tree house. She climbs the ladder and goes inside. She sticks her blonde head out the window. *Please stay in that tree house. Please just stay right there.*

I haven't been this horror-struck since Max Adams started chasing me that day in the forest. It all feels like a really bad dream and I keep praying that this is a really bad dream and that I'm still sleeping in the Walmart parking lot because I have a really bad feeling that this is about to end in hellfire.

Thomas approaches the tree house. He sees his sister through the window. "Gotcha!" He lunges for the ladder but she climbs down it just before he gets there. She runs a big circle around the tree house. At one point she's only about ten feet from the hole. I can't breathe. She giggles. Thomas laughs. He's almost caught her. Olivia backs up and goes the other way, tricking him. She runs an even bigger circle around the tree house and then… *crrrunnnch*. There's the sound like the breaking of a thousand bones as the stick covering splinters apart. A moment later, Thomas is screaming his head off and that's when I know that Max's tiny blonde daughter is dead.

"Olivia!" Thomas cries, staring down into the hole, his face a ruin. He runs away, back toward the house. In absolute terror, I approach the hole. What I see there will haunt me for the rest of my life.

There, laying atop all the broken sticks and twigs, facedown, is an unmoving Olivia. There's blood everywhere and the way one knife is positioned I think it's going right through her face. I start shaking all over.

I did this.

I turn away, unable to stomach the sight of her for another second. I hear footsteps approaching. I hide behind a new tree. I watch Max's wife peer into the hole, though I can't make out much detail, the scene all blurry through my tears. She falls to her knees in utter silence, too stunned to cry. Max is behind her. He looks into the hole and starts calling out "Olivia! Olivia!" in the most broken way, tears rushing down his face. The son sits atop a pile of autumn leaves, rocking back and forth with his legs tucked into his chest, wailing.

I sink down to my knees against the trunk of the tree. The Adams' sobbing is so loud. It's like they're screaming right in my ear. They stay there for a while until they leave to call the police I assume. I head back to my Subaru.

My hands are trembling as I drive out of the Adams' suburb. I drive an hour out of town for no reason at all. Every time I blink, I see Max's daughter and her blonde hair soaked with blood. I can't even fathom how to go on living my life after this. I just killed a little girl. I just killed a little girl with a dozen steak knives and I can't undo it. I can't take it back.

I go to Walmart. I buy a new pair of sneakers and dispose of my old ones in some random alley dumpster. I get back in my car, drive for a minute or so, then turn into a strip mall parking lot. I sit in the driver's seat and bawl my eyes out until it feels like I have no more tears to cry.

Eventually, I head back home. When I walk through the front door, Tiff and Ang are sitting on the couch just like they were when I left. For a moment, it's nice to pretend that no time had passed, that my life hadn't been irrevocably changed in the span of a single day, that I hadn't fucked up a family forever. Tiff and Ang barely notice me walk in, which makes things easier but then Angela says, "did your delivery driver friend have a girl or boy?"

I want to start screaming. I want to tear all of our cheap furniture apart and tear the cheap prints of famous paintings from our walls but instead, I say "a little girl, a beautiful little girl". I hang my head, walk upstairs and hope Ang and Tiff hadn't seen the tears in my eyes.

Fifteen

That night, in the few and far between moments I'm actually asleep, I dream of a thick slab of exposed flesh laying on the ground. It looks like a hunk of a dead manatee or something, all blubbery. It has all these marks through it, deep, straight cuts like Etch A Sketch lines, welling with blood.

I wake up in a cold sweat. I'm breathing heavy. It wakes up Ang. She rolls over to face me. "What's wrong?"

"Just a bad dream," I say. I have no idea what the dream meant. I'm guessing it's just some fucked up abstraction of Olivia's death, though the block of flesh was much too wide to belong to a little girl. It looked like a torso, a much meatier, musclier back. "Go back to sleep," I tell Ang.

She huffs and turns away from me. Years ago, she would never have turned away from me. She would have cuddled into me, told me it would all be okay.

I get out of bed, go downstairs to the kitchen. I pour myself a glass of water. My hand shakes around the glass. Water isn't going to cut it. I open our liquor cabinet and get out a good bottle of scotch an old buddy had bought me for my birthday, back when I had the time and energy for friends. I'd been saving it for something I guess, a celebration of sorts, for the Big Miraculous Change I'd always prayed for. Well, it was here now. Let's raise a glass to the newest card-carrying member of Child Murderers of America!

I take a swig straight from the bottle. It burns my throat like a branding iron. I can't get enough. I pace around the living room with the bottle in my hand, taking sip after sip, drifting further and further from reality. I try my best not to think about the Adams—how they're probably up right now, pacing around their big fancy house with tears in their eyes, knowing their world will never be the same—but I think of nothing but the Adams. At one point, Olivia appears like an apparition before me, her one blue eye blinking, the other replaced by the handle of a knife. The eye socket wound crying blood.

I should kill myself. I *will* kill myself. Right now. This is the only good decision I've made in years. I start fumbling around our kitchen drawers, those junk drawers no one ever cleans out, looking for pills to overdose on. There are old packets of Advil, a small bottle of Tylenol, some aspirin. I know Ang keeps her Zoloft in the bathroom cabinet. "What's with all the noise?" It's Tiffany. She's standing midway down the stairs in an old sleeping t-shirt, her hair up in a bun.

I quickly shut the drawer I'm rifling through with my hip. "Can't sleep," I say, trying my best not to slur.

"Are you drunk, dad?" Tiffany asks, eyeing the half-empty bottle of scotch on the kitchen counter. She walks downstairs. I think she'll yell at me, or roll her eyes in disgust at her loser dad the way she always does, but by some miracle, she actually seems concerned. "Are you okay, dad?" she asks in a soft voice.

"What?"

"Why are you up drinking at 4 a.m.? You barely even drink."

"I'm fine, Tiff, just go to sleep." I place a hand on my throbbing head and close my eyes. "Go back to bed sweetie, pretend this was a dream."

"Alright." She turns away and goes back upstairs. I grab the bottle of scotch from the counter and bring it into the living room. I plop down on the couch and fall fast asleep before I remember that I was supposed to kill myself.

Sixteen

"I hope they find that god-awful killer."

"What?"

Ang is in the kitchen unloading the dishwasher. She points at the TV with a fork in her hand. "The one who killed that poor little girl."

I snap out of my I-just-murdered-a-child daze and lock eyes with the literal child I've just murdered on the news. It's a picture of Olivia from her third-grade yearbook, her blonde hair pulled back in a headband, her big blue eyes all twinkly. I jump a little. "Jesus," I mutter.

"What?" Ang says.

"I... yeah... I hope they find him too." The TV cuts to filmed footage of my booby trap, the knives stained with blood, and I find myself wondering how the hell the coroners dislodged Olivia's body, and if the rest of the Adams stayed to watch. *One of the knives went right through her eye, hitting a major artery*, the reporter states. *She died almost instantly.* "I'm gonna go outside for a minute," I say. I get up from the couch and go outside. I start pacing around our porch and breathing really heavy. I guess you could call it hyperventilating. Seconds later, I throw up all over the dewy grass in front of our porch steps. I wipe my mouth on the sleeve of my housecoat, the blue sky spinning.

I'm back inside the house just in time to catch a glimpse of an adorable home video of Olivia picking apples on Max's shoulders, her mother and brother trotting happily behind them. The video cuts to live footage of Max and his wife and son standing on their front lawn. Max's face is red with anger and Max's wife is crying. She looks like she's aged ten years in a single night. Thomas is staring just past the camera with all these tears dried on his freckled face, the wind blowing back his brown hair. "We won't stop until we find who did this," Max says into the camera. It's like he's staring straight at me.

Ang shakes her head. "Horrible," she says, putting the last of the plates away.

"Why do you watch that stuff? It only brings you down. You know I've always hated watching the news," I say. I take a sip from the glass of orange juice I've been nursing for over an hour, but it fails to mask the puke taste that clings to my tongue like barnacles to a boat.

Ang puts a hand on her hip. "It's called compassion."

"How the heck does watching someone else's misfortune on TV equal compassion? The only reason people watch the news is to confirm that people have got it worse off than they do, period."

"Yeah, because our life is just so goddamn depressing, right Rex?" She rolls her eyes.

I don't answer. Since finding me passed out on the couch with that bottle of scotch earlier this morning, I can tell she's in the mood to fight. I'm kind of in the mood to fight too. There's so much I want to say to her, so many things I want to ask her, namely, who are you, you pancake-titted, sexless old woman, and what did you do with my wife, did you eat her?

Sometimes, I hate Ang. The new Ang. The grumbly, unlikeable Ang who smells of talcum powder and the rotting of her soul. The Ang with bags beneath her eyes like squishy ketchup packets. Sometimes, I want to prick those bags with a needle. I have a theory that those bags hold all the tears she's refused to cry, all the sadness she's stored away, and if I cut them open she'd cry forever but I'd be happy, or happier, because at least it meant she was feeling something.

Tiff comes downstairs in this very nice dress I'd never seen before, or at least it would be a very nice dress on someone thinner. On her, it just looks like a curtain tied around a Mrs. Potato Head doll. I know that's really mean, but that's what people have brains for, to think really mean things they'd never say and in turn, can't be blamed for. "New dress?" I ask.

Tiff nods. "Yeah, mom got it for me."

"That's nice, what was the occasion?"

"Just cuz," Tiff says, her eyes down.

"Because you stomped all over her phone, Rex," Ang says.

"Mom!" Tiff says. Her chins start wobbling. "Don't, he'll be mad."

"So we went to the mall to buy her a new one, and we saw the dress in a shop window and I figured she deserved it after all the stress you put her through," Ang says.

71

My hands form fists. I know Ang wanted me to blow up, so I stay as cool as a cucumber. "Terrific," I say through gritted teeth.

"Do you like it, dad?" Tiff asks. It's so out of character for her to even care what I think that it softens me up a little.

"You look beautiful, kid," I say, but it's a lie, because I don't think the sort of morbid obesity that means you'll die at forty can ever be beautiful, but Tiff's face is pretty, it really is, so I thought I'd tell her. "You have such a pretty face, sweetie."

Her chins start wobbling again. "Don't say that, dad." Tears fill her eyes.

"Rex!" Ang says all mad at me.

"Jesus, what'd I say?"

"You don't tell a plus-size girl she's got a pretty face, Rex, everyone knows that," Ang says. "You just tell her she's pretty, that *all* of her is pretty."

I sigh. "Well, I'm sorry no one provided me with a handbook." God, I'm pissed. Pissed that Ang got Tiff a phone again so she could turn right back into a zombie, pissed that Ang lets Tiff eat whatever she wants all the time. Am I the only one who cares? I turn to Tiff. "Tiff, I know you hate when I bring this up but, honey, you need to lose weight. It's a matter of health at this point, and it doesn't have anything to do with you as a person, or how beautiful you are, I just... I want you to be around for a long time and I'm worr—"

"Just stop it!" Tiff says. "I just want you to say I'm pretty dad. I... I like this dress. I know you're embarrassed of me, but would it kill you, for once in your life, to just not comment on my weight?"

"Jesus, sweetie, I'm not embarrassed of you!" I say, but sadly, I am embarrassed of her, just like how Timmy's dad was embarrassed of Timmy's brother, just like how my dad was embarrassed of me. What can I say? I'm a terrible person. I'm child-murdering scum.

"Yes, you are," Tiff says, her voice catching. "I can feel it, dad." She runs upstairs crying.

"Nice going, Rex," Ang says. She's frying up bacon for Tiff to help slowly kill her. I'm struck with the urge to grab the skillet from the stove and club Ang over the head with it like a seal. I think about Max and his family and how they're always drinking green drinks and eating vegetables and lean protein and how Max runs every night at 8 p.m. on the dot and how his daughter went to gymnastics and karate four times a week and how his son is probably the star of his soccer team and how the wife rides her Peloton bike every morning in the living room by the big bay window that overlooks Lake Michigan and how they are so much better than we are, how they are so much smarter and better looking and more successful, and how I miss watching them, and how I want to be them. "Go apologize to Tiffany," Ang says, bacon grease sizzling and spattering in a sort of rhythm, like a song by a band called Heart Disease.

"Sure," I say. "But you're planning her funeral, Ang, when she dies at thirty-eight from diabetes, or a goddamn heart attack, so have fun with that."

Ang sighs. "I can't deal with you today. You're too much."

"Yeah," I say under my breath. "Alright, then. I'm too much." I settle back into the couch and change the channel so I don't have to look at Olivia anymore.

Seventeen

That night, I lie wide awake in bed next to a sleeping Ang. I want to be far away from her. So far away from this house, this life. Far from Tiffany and her growing collection of chins. Most of all, I want to be far away—far removed—from myself. I get out of bed at around 1 a.m., quietly open our closet door, and take out some jeans, a flannel shirt, and some socks. I change in the bathroom. I'm set on drinking myself into oblivion at some hole-in-the-wall bar, maybe dying of alcohol poisoning if it's in the cards.

I head outside and get in the car. I start it, turn out of the driveway, and lo and behold, there's Tiff in that new dress, her trademark whore makeup and an open grey coat. She's walking toward the house. What the hell? She sees me. She freezes. An elephant in the headlights. She doesn't look alright. All this eyeliner had run down her face like she'd been crying. "Tiff?" I roll down the window.

"Dad?" She walks up to the car. "Dad, don't be mad at me."

"Where were you?"

"At a party... at Caroline's. Please don't ground me."

"Who drove you there?"

"Ash and Erin."

"Did they drive you home?"

"No. I... I walked home."

My heart palpitates. "Tiff, Caroline's must be two miles from here. Something could have happened to you! You could have been raped!"

"I know, it was stupid. I'm... I'm okay. Sorry."

I blow air out of my cheeks. "Well, I'm so glad you're okay, Tiff."

"Are you?" she asks, her voice whiny. "Or do you wish I'd just die?" She starts crying. I can tell she's drunk.

"What? Tiff, get in the car." She walks over to the passenger side and gets in. "Tiff, I love you. I'm just worried about your health."

She nods. "I know, I know. I'm worried about it too." She looks up at me through a mess of fake eyelashes. For a second, her face looks just like it did as a baby's, minus all the makeup.

"Oh, Tiff." I lean forward and hug her. She cries on my shoulder. "I love you so much, okay?" I say.

"It doesn't feel like it."

"I'm sorry, I'm so sorry, Tiff."

"Am I grounded?"

"No, sweetie, you're not grounded."

"Are you going to tell mom?"

"I don't think she needs to know."

"Yeah," Tiff says, sniffling. "She's sad enough already."

"So you see it too?"

"What?"

"Your mother's sadness?"

"Yeah dad, I think anyone could see it. I think it could be seen from a satellite."

"Well, what should we do?"

Tiff shrugs. "I don't know."

"Alright Tiff, since you're not being grounded, why don't you make me a deal?"

"A deal?"

"Yeah."

"What is it?"

"Let's fix this family, Tiff. Let's... let's do things together, not just watch TV. Let's go on Sunday drives, and maybe we could start something, all three of us, like an art class or something. And maybe we could start exercising, Tiff, just a little bit. Not just for you Tiff, your mom and I aren't exactly in the best shape either."

She smiles a little. "Alright, dad. Deal."

I kiss the top of her head. "That's my girl."

"Dad, where were you going by the way?"

I start the car again so I can turn it around, park in the driveway and go back inside our house, our home. "Doesn't matter," I say.

Eighteen

Ang always has the news on in the living room, bubbling in the background like boiling water. Olivia has been dead for a week now, and the fear never relents. Days ago, I almost got into a car wreck when I damn near swerved off the road at the sight of an approaching cop car. Every day, I expect the police to knock on the door after unearthing some sort of evidence I'd carelessly left in my wake. The suspense is slowly killing me. The only thing keeping me going is the deal I made with Tiff and it's fucked up that I'd robbed Max of a daughter only to gain back mine, but I guess Max Adams bashing me over the head with a rock and raping me in the ass is fucked up too, so maybe we're even.

Since killing Olivia, I do a lot of thinking. A lot of reflecting. Sometimes I walk around at night amidst streetlights and stars and just wonder. I wonder about a lot of things. I wonder about who I'd be, who I would have become if I'd never met Max Adams.

I also wonder a lot about Max. I do a lot of speculating, which ultimately leads to nothing, but is sort of comforting in a way. I wonder about his home life when he was a kid.

Sometimes I imagine different scenarios that could have led to him being so fucked up. Like maybe he was gay, and when he tried to come out to his parents, his dad beat him to a pulp and made him swear to stay in the closet for the rest of his life. Or maybe he himself had been raped. Or maybe, he'd just been born an asshole, with an anger inside him so bloodthirsty it couldn't be contained.

That's how I've felt since the day Max Adams raped me. Like I housed an anger that was bigger than myself. Like my bones were breaking just trying to keep it inside. There is a violence inside me. An ever-present undercurrent of rage. It slithers beneath my skin. Buried, but there. Sometimes, I scare myself. Like the other morning, when I was mad at Ang and wanted to club her over the head with that skillet. Is it normal to think thoughts like that about your own wife? Is it normal to wish she was dead, if only for one white-hot minute?

When I first saw Max Adams and his preppy, perfect family at the gas station, my first thought was that I couldn't believe his life just went on. I couldn't believe that he kept breathing, kept waking up every morning. Kept eating and working. Kept trying and living, after what he'd done to me. But now, since killing Olivia, I see that life really does just go on. Think about it: the most traumatic thing you've ever lived through, the sexual abuse, the divorce, the affair, the time you got food poisoning and shit yourself in the mall, that time you kissed someone and they didn't kiss you back, th`e time you filed bankruptcy, the racist joke you told while drunk at a dinner party. God, if we carried all that with us, we'd never get out of bed in the morning. So like a mole, we bury it. We have to.

Yesterday, Ang, Tiff, and I went on a run. Okay, so it was more like a fast walk, but we still broke a sweat. It was a start. And on the fast walk, we passed a corner store, and I walked in and proudly bought three green drinks, the same brand that the Adams buy. Tiff pinched her nose shut the whole time she drank it, but she agreed to have a few a week, and that made me smile for the first time in so long. Ang even seemed to enjoy hers.

Ang and I talked about Tiffany's phone use, and we agreed that she should only be allowed to use it for an hour a day. When we broke the news to Tiffany, she wasn't even mad. "Okay," she said. "Sounds fair." Ang and I couldn't believe it. We were so happy, that night, we even had sex.

It's funny, I'm starting to miss spying on the Adams less and less, and sometimes, I go a full hour without thinking of them. When I do think of them, it's a guilt-ridden hell, of course, but the in-between moments make living worthwhile.

"You look nice, honey," I say to Ang. "Real nice."

She brightens. "Yeah?" She's wearing a black dress, red lipstick, my mother's pearls. She even has high heels on, two inches but still, it's something. We're going to a restaurant, a nice restaurant. This little Italian place in town where fancy rich people like Max go. I can tell Ang is excited. I can't take credit. It was Tiff's idea. "You should take mom on a date," she told me yesterday while she was reading a book—yes, a *book*—on the couch.

"So, how's work?" I ask Ang when we're seated at the table, a candle flame flickering between us.

"Oh, it's fine. It's work," she says. She scans the menu. "Shrimp scampi sounds good, don't you think?"

"Sounds incredible."

She smiles. "You're in a good mood."

"I'm out with a beautiful woman, why wouldn't I be in a good mood?"

"Oh my, do you think you're getting lucky again tonight?" She raises an eyebrow.

"I mean, I better be, the shrimp scampi is thirty-nine dollars."

She laughs.

We eat dinner, which is delicious. We're full and happy and wine-drunk. It's wonderful. We reminisce about the early days, back when everything felt possible. Maybe everything still is possible. At one point in the night, I use the restroom, and while I'm washing my hands, the guy staring back at me in the mirror doesn't look too bad. I'd lost a few pounds this week out of sheer worry, and the red wine had put color in my cheeks and my white button-down shirt fit me pretty nice. "You're alright, Rex Constanzo," I say to the guy in the mirror, still pretty tipsy. "You're alright."

Nineteen

I wake up the next morning feeling absolutely disgusted with myself. I can't believe I'd let myself spend over two hundred dollars on some stupid dinner and pretend like everything was okay when I've just murdered a child. I think I was still in shock, or the thick of denial. But I'm out of it now. The bubble has burst. This morning, I think about the Adams so much it's like they're right here beside me. Like they're my shadow or something. What have I done to that family? On the news, Max's beautiful wife still looks a decade older, and Thomas will probably wind up being a school shooter or something from all this trauma, how could he not? I mean, look what I'd done because of what his dad did to me, what heinous crime I'd committed. If I've learned anything from all this, it's that Timmy's hot potato analogy makes a lot of sense: hate has to go somewhere, it can't just stay locked up inside.

Olivia's funeral was yesterday. I need to say goodbye to her. Tell her how sorry I am. I think seeing her gravestone and really letting what I'd done sink in—become concrete rather than the distanced, amorphous thing it had numbed to—might give me some closure. And maybe, eventually, that closure would become a kind of peace. I think it's an important step because, as cruel a truth as it is, there's not a single thing I can do to bring Olivia back. She's gone, and my own family needs me now.

Ang is at work, and Tiff is at school but I have the day off, so I head out to the cemetery. I don't think going is too risky, because Timmy's buried there too. Besides, just about the whole town had gone to pay their respects to Olivia. It would probably seem more suspicious if I don't go.

On the news, I saw Olivia's grave was covered with just about a billion teddy bears and bouquets. When Timmy died, no one gave him a teddy bear or a bouquet, I guess because he was just some skinny poor kid and no one really cared, but the Adams are rich and beautiful, and everyone knows that being rich and beautiful means people care. A few weeks after Timmy died, his mother let me go through his room in case I wanted to keep anything, and I took back the shark kite I'd given him. That night, I dug a little hole by his grave and buried it beside him.

I pull into the cemetery and pull right back out when I see the Adams' BMW in the parking lot, and what's left of the Adams huddled nearby. God, I'm an idiot, an even bigger idiot than I previously thought I was. This idea was so stupid, and it *was* risky. Saying goodbye wouldn't give me an ounce of closure, or peace. I was a child murderer for God's sake! That's not really something you can run away from.

I swear Thomas saw me through my windshield. Recognized me. His eyes bore right into mine. There was no reason why the Adams wouldn't have suspected me; the strange, sinister man who followed them to a campsite and ruined their weekend. They probably *had* suspected me but didn't remember my name, didn't know where I lived, or how to find me. Of course, Max remembers my name, but I think he's too afraid to speak it. If Max has suspected me all along, I think he's been keeping it to himself, scared that I'd tell the police about the rape. Of course, there was no proof the rape happened, no DNA or anything. And it was so long ago. All I would have is my word against his. But everyone knows that words like that wield tremendous power, especially in this day and age. If I went public with it, no one would ever look at Max Adams the same way again. There would always be a question in their eyes, a quake in their hearts. To accuse someone of rape is to condemn them to a lifetime imprisonment in others' doubt, no matter the verdict.

But if the Adams had seen me at the cemetery, they could be almost sure that I was Olivia's killer, and any rape allegations would never hold water, especially if the police could prove that I was guilty, which I'm sure they can. The Adams had me now. If Thomas really had recognized me, my license plate had been his for the taking. Or, just like I had followed them, the Adams could be following me in their BMW right now.

God, what had I done? I think I want to get caught. Deep down, I want to get caught. Life has been too good lately, much too good for a man who's just murdered a child and I can't take it. I don't deserve it. So I'd sabotaged it. It's clear as day. The only thing worse than being caught for a crime is not being caught for a crime. The guilt is a prison all its own.

I should turn myself in. I should drive straight to the police station and turn myself in. That would be the noble thing to do. The right thing. But Tiff and Ang, they love me now. They'd be so upset. Tiff would eat her feelings, become even fatter, and die at twenty-five. And she's doing so well. She'd even agreed to go on another fast walk to the green juice store after school today. If I turn myself in or kill myself, I know it would slowly kill her too, and then two innocent young girls would be dead instead of one.

Twenty

Days go by and nothing changes. The only thing that's changed is that I'm no longer able to enjoy my life, even for a second. I go through the motions, go on our fast walks, make our healthier dinners, watch our movies, but inside, I'm splitting apart. Thomas Adams' eyes are all I see, the same cold blue eyes as his father's.

On the fifth day since the cemetery visit, something strange happens. I'm going outside to get the mail, and right on our welcome mat is a bag of pork rinds, a store-bought kind with a smiling cartoon pig on the front. I bend down to pick it up. Is this some sort of promotion, some free sample from a local grocery store? If it is, I find the choice of pork rinds bizarre given the kosher and vegan/vegetarian populations. Isn't business nowadays all about inclusion? I work for a potato chip company, I think I know a thing or two about the food industry.

I flip over the bag. There's a Post-it note attached, with the words *Oink! Oink!* written in permanent marker. I really don't know what to make of this. If it's a threat from the Adams, it's a tepid one, and I really don't understand it. I decide to chalk it up to nothing.

I head back inside with the bag of pork rinds and throw them out, because no one here is eating them. We're healthy now.

Twenty-One

It's been two days since the pork rinds, and I've mostly forgotten all about them. I'm trying to turn over a new leaf because I have to believe that if Thomas Adams really had recognized me, the Adams would have taken action by now. If Max Adams had killed Tiff, I would have gutted him like a fish already.

Speaking of Tiff, the reason I'm trying to turn over a new leaf is so I can really be there for her, so I can be the best dad I possibly can be because, when I knocked on Tiff's bedroom door tonight to tell her that dinner was ready, she was crying. "What's wrong, honey?" I asked.

She sniffled, shrugged. "Nothing."

"You can tell me."

She sighed. "Oh, I just hate myself sometimes."

I walked over to her and put a hand on her shoulder. "Honey, don't say that. You're a terrific young lady, you should be really proud of yourself."

"No, I'm not, dad. You... you don't know the half of it, you... you don't understand. You could never understand."

"Well try me, sweetie." I crouched down beside her. I looked deep into her eyes, which were floating in a sea of black, bleeding makeup.

"I... I'm just having a fight, with Caroline, and some of the other girls."

"About what?"

"Oh, you know, just silly girl stuff."

"You sure that's what this is about, Tiff?"

She nodded, but she could no longer look at me. "Yeah, dad, I'm sure."

I stood back up but before I left, I said, "you know, Tiff, when I was your age, I was going through a lot of things, things no one knew about, things no one *knows* about."

"What do you mean?"

I raked a hand through my barely-there hair. "I just mean that being a teenager... being a *person*, it's a lot."

She nodded. "Yeah, it is."

"You can tell me anything, sweetie, anything at all. At any time."

She smiled wanly. "Thanks dad."

"No problem, honey."

I went back downstairs. Ang was setting the table and the meatloaf in the oven was just about done. "Where's Tiff?" she asked. "Didn't you tell her to come down for dinner?"

"She's not feeling well."

"What do you mean?"

"She's crying."

"Why?"

"I don't really know."

"Well tell her to get her butt down here, you just spent an hour making that meatloaf."

"That's okay, Ang. She doesn't have to come down if she doesn't want to. I'll bring her up a plate."

Ang put a hand on her hip. "I'm not babying her, Rex. Her parents just made her dinner, she has to come downstairs and eat it. That's the way it works."

"Says who?"

"Huh?"

"She's sad tonight, Ang. Why does she have to come downstairs? She's obviously going through something."

"She's just being dramatic, probably a ploy for attention, or another new dress."

"Ang." There was a catch in my throat, and then tears in my eyes. "When I was her age, I was going through so much, so much that no one could see. And God, I wish somebody would have cared, would have just asked me what was wrong."

Ang crossed her arms. "Are you seriously crying, Rex?"

My cheeks burned hot with shame. What the hell had gotten into me?

I quickly wiped my tears away. I tried to laugh it off. "That time of the month, I suppose."

"I'll say," Ang said. "Jesus, what a weird night." She placed the last of the cutlery on the table and folded the napkins. "When your balls descend, could you tell Tiff to come down for dinner?"

"Yeah," I said. "Of course."

Twenty-Two

After forcing a teary-eyed Tiff through dinner, I feel depressed as anything, and not just because I'm a child murderer. It's because we're no longer changing. Our family isn't getting better anymore, I can feel it. Ang is back to her bitchy self, and Tiff is sad and unmotivated, lying on the couch and scrolling her phone. "It's been over an hour," I say to Tiff, wiping down the kitchen counters.

"Oh, come on, dad, just this once."

"What do you like about it?"

"Like about what?"

"The phone."

She looks up at me. "Honestly?"

"Yeah."

"It... it helps me forget."

"Forget what?"

"About being some nobody fat girl in middle America."

"Tiff!"

"I'm serious dad!" She sits up. She grabs a big chunk of her belly fat through her pajamas. "I mean, look at this, dad. Imagine... imagine having to carry this around every day, walk through the halls with this attached to me. Everyone stares at me."

"You don't think I know what that feels like?" I say, pointing to my limpy-leg. "Kids used to call me Gimpy every single day of my life."

"And how did that make you feel?"

"Invisible."

"Well, you're lucky, dad. All I want is to disappear, but I'm like a blimp. You can't not see me. And at the same time, all I want is to be seen, but seen as something else I guess, *someone* else. When I see all these gorgeous people on Instagram, living these amazing lives I guess it's like an escape for a bit. It's like running away."

I rinse the dishcloth beneath the sink and wash and dry my hands. I'm amazed by how much she's willing to open up to me. Maybe she and I are more similar than I thought: we're both out-of-our minds desperate for someone to talk to. I go over to the couch and sit beside her. "I want you to live a life you don't have to run away from, Tiff. But sometimes the only way out is through. I really do want to help you lose weight. Let's go on a run, or a fast walk, tomorrow after school."

"Alright." She's quiet for a while before she says, "thanks, dad."

"For what?"

"For listening."

Twenty-Three

In my dream that night, I'm back staring down at that mystery torso with all the bloody Etch A Sketch cuts. I wake up clammy. I creep out of bed and down the stairs. I go into the kitchen and grab the half-empty bottle of scotch from the liquor cabinet. I make my way over to the living room couch. I stop. There's someone in the front yard.

I set down the bottle of scotch. Heart hammering, I fling open the front door. The silhouetted figure doesn't budge.

The porch lights flicker on. The figure reveals itself: a severed pig's head on a wooden post. I go cold. Unlike that bag of pork rinds, there's no possible way that I can chalk this up to nothing.

I run down to the basement and get out my gun from the gun safe. I hadn't held it in years, since the fifteenth anniversary of my rape and Timmy's death, when I'd driven to Lake Michigan and fired it over the water a half-dozen times. After what Max Adams did to me, I promised myself I'd get a gun when I was older, especially if I one day had a family to protect. I never wanted to feel that helpless again.

I take the gun upstairs, go into the garage, and get a tarp. I put my coat on and stash my gun in my coat pocket, grab our emergency flashlight, the car keys, and put on my snow boots. It had snowed for the first time last night and that had taken me out of my depression for a bit, watching the snowflakes fall, but all the snow did tonight was take me back to that day in the forest, the day I felt the same brand of unbridled terror I was feeling now. The Adams know. The Adams know everything. *Max* Adams knows everything.

I walk outside and over to the pig's head. I'm well aware that this could be a trap, that Max Adams could fly out of the bushes with a steak knife and stab me to death, but it's not like I can leave this here. I grab the wooden post below the pig's shorn neck, trying my best to keep my eyes up so I don't have to look at its face, whose own eyes had been plucked out of its head. God, it stinks. I imagine it smells like an exhumed casket being opened, the body inside reduced to a gelatinous bisque.

I wrap it in the tarp and throw it in the back of my Subaru, all the while looking over my shoulder like a nervous bird. I drive with all the windows open, even though it's ice cold outside, just to try to cope with the smell. I drive for a long time before I reach an out-of-town dumpster and throw the whole mess away. On the drive home, I wrack my brain for what this whole pig theme means. The only pig reference I can think of is from the movie *Deliverance*, where the man is told to "squeal like a pig" while he's being raped by another man. That has to be it. I remember seeing the movie with Angela when we were in our twenties. Ang had rented it from the video store and we'd ordered pizza. When that scene came around my heart was like thunder in my ears and I excused myself to the bathroom and threw up in the toilet. I still remember a lone, whole pepperoni floating around the toilet bowl after I flushed.

Twenty-Four

That night, my dreams twist through rows of noose-necked Timmys hung from branches like Christmas tree ornaments. Images flash like fireworks, the pig's head, the booby trap, Olivia's blood-soaked hair. The mystery torso. The flash of Max Adams' pocketknife.

"Wake up! Rex, wake up!"

"Huh?" I crack open my eyes to see the foggy figure of Ang standing over me in the blue-dark of our bedroom, shaking my shoulder. The sheets around me are wet. "What's going on?"

"Jesus, you tell me. You were having a nightmare I assume. Or more than a nightmare. It was like a night terror. At one point, you were screaming. I thought you might even wake up Tiff."

I sit up and wipe my sweaty face on the comforter. "God, I... I don't know."

"Do you remember what it was about?"

"No... I... I don't know."

Ang opens the blinds to our bedroom windows, the pale, 7 a.m. sun filtering in. "Would you like some water?"

"Okay, sure."

Ang disappears into our bathroom and returns with a glass

of tap water. "Thanks," I say, taking a sip before setting it down on the nightstand.

"You should have seen yourself, Rex. You were shaking like a leaf. I'd never seen anything like—"

Tiff screams.

Ang runs out of the room. I scramble out of bed in my drenched pajamas and follow, my heart slamming against my ribcage. Ang bursts through Tiff's bedroom door. Tiff is hysterical, standing at the edge of her bed and staring out her bedroom window. "What the fuck?" she says. "What the actual fuck?"

Tiff's window is splattered in what appears to be blood or red paint, almost completely covered by it. Pig's blood, I presume. I race out of her room, grab my gun from beneath my side of the mattress, and run down the stairs and outside. I hide my gun between my hip bone and the elastic loop of my pajama pants because Tiff and Ang don't even know I own a gun. I stand in the snowy front yard, look up at our house, and see that the only window coated in blood is Tiffany's. A chill runs through me. I guess Thomas Adams had recognized me after all. This proves it. It also proves that Max Adams doesn't want to involve the police. He wants to take matters into his own hands. An eye for an eye. A daughter for a daughter. This has become a sick, twisted game to Max Adams. A game he's winning.

The front door flies open. It's Tiff.

"Get back inside!" I say.

"Dad!"

"Now!"

She closes the door. I check all around our property. I check the bushes and the garage. We're being watched. I can feel it.

I go back inside.

"Shouldn't we call the police?" Ang asks me.

Tiff is sitting in a corner of the living room, biting her nails. "Caroline's mad at me," she says quietly.

"What?"

"I'm sorry. I'm so sorry. I think it was Caroline. We... we had a fight. I think it's a prank. I'm sorry to scare you, to wake you up like that," Tiff says.

"Tiff, do you really think Caroline could be angry enough to throw blood-red paint up at your window? That seems sociopathic," Ang says.

"Teenage girls can be sociopathic, I assure you," Tiff says. "Caroline especially." I believed her. Of all Tiff's stupid slutty friends, Caroline was by far the worst. Caroline was a bitch. A bully. She was loud and obnoxious. She cussed in every conversation, even around parents. She was a real wild child.

"So that's it then?" I say, partly relieved. I didn't believe it had been Caroline for a second, but if Tiff and Ang did, then I could take care of things on my own, without the two of them breathing down my neck. "You really think it was just some stupid prank?"

Tiff nods. "Yeah, sorry."

"Well alright then, that's some way to start the day," I say.

Ang rolls her eyes. "Jesus," she says. "Well, whatever you

did, Tiff, you better make it up to her, or she might murder you."
I shiver involuntarily at the word murder.

"Trust me, I deserve it," Tiff says.

"Why? What did you do?" I ask.

Tiff sighs. "It's just a stupid girl fight, dad. She'll get over it."

"I should call her mother, tell her Caroline defaced our home," Ang says. "I'll definitely send them the bill. We'll have to get the wall beneath your window repainted, you know. And I have no idea how we're going to get the paint off the window." Ang turns to me. "Rex, will we have to get a new window?"

"I'll pay for it," Tiff says. "With the birthday money grandma gave me. You can have it... all of it. I'm really sorry."

"You don't have to do that," I say. "We'll take care of it, honey."

"Rex!" Ang says, "what about teaching her responsibility?"

I wish I could say that I'm responsible, that I'm responsible for all of it, that if I'd never stopped for that gas station donut and coffee all those months ago, none of this would be happening. An innocent little girl wouldn't be dead. Except I'm not sure if I'm responsible, or if Max Adams is responsible. Had I started all of this, or had he? When did the hating start, and when would it stop? Would it ever stop? "Keep your birthday money, Tiff. We'll take care of it," I say. I cut Angela a look. She rolls her eyes again.

"Well, I'm calling Caroline's mother," Ang says.

Tiffany's eyes widen. "Mom, don't! Don't!" She stands up. "Just... I'll pay for it. Just don't call her mom, okay?"

"Fine, but this all seems a little fishy, Tiff. What are you hiding?" Ang says with her trademark angry-mother-hand-on-the-hip.

"Let's let her have some privacy, Ang. She can work things out with her friend herself. For God's sake, she's seventeen years old. She's not a little kid anymore. We don't need to know everything," I say.

Tiff looks at me, relieved. "Thanks, dad."

"And we'll pay for it, sweetie," I say.

"Whatever," Ang says, leaving the room.

"Dad?" Tiff says.

"Yeah?"

"Thanks for standing up for me." She walks over and hugs me. I turn my body away from hers a little so she doesn't notice the gun. "You're a good dad and... and even with all the stuff about my weight, or the phone or whatever, I know it's because you love me. I know you're just trying to help me. So thanks. It... it means a lot."

I smile, my heart all warm and fuzzy. "Don't mention it, kiddo."

"Can I ask you something though, dad?"

"Yeah."

She gulps. "Why all of a sudden?"

"All of a sudden what?"

"Well, it's like... lately it's like you've sparked to life. It's like you're intent on winning a World's Greatest Dad trophy or something. It just seems... a little manic."

"Manic?"

"Yeah."

I scratch the back of my neck, my heart no longer all warm and fuzzy but cold, vestigial, corroded with frost. She sees right through me. "I'm trying to make up for lost time, I guess. I've spent a lot of my life in a sort of fog."

"Why do you think?"

Well, sweetie, when I was around your age, I was raped in the ass by the captain of the football team, and now I've gone and killed his only daughter on a bed of knives... "Did I ever tell you about my friend Timmy?"

"I don't think so."

"Wait, Tiff, can we... can we go on a drive? Spend some time together? It's the weekend after all."

She smiles. "I'll get dressed."

Twenty-Five

I feel obligated to invite Ang on Tiff and my car trip, so I do. She says no, and that she has a headache from "all this drama". I'm relieved that she and her bitchiness won't be tagging along, telling us to turn the car radio down, or that we were talking too loudly. Ang is lying on the couch watching the news, rubbing her temples and intermittently sighing. I've noticed that Olivia's death is beginning to take up less and less airtime, and I guess I would have believed this whole thing was simmering down if I hadn't stumbled into last night's porcine purgatory.

Tiff walks downstairs, dressed in jeans and a black sweater. The sweater is the most flattering thing she owns. I know, because I ordered it online for her last Christmas after Googling "flattering clothes for fat girls" in incognito mode on our computer. I hate that she's wearing it. I know she's wearing it because she wants to earn my approval, which isn't something that should have to be earned. God, I'm a piece of shit. The way my father treated me growing up—the disgusted looks and the insults thinly veiled as jokes—helped me turn into the sad excuse for a man I am today. I'm no better of a father than he is. I might be even worse. The line between genuinely wanting to help Tiff and simply using her to distract me from the fact that I've just murdered a child is blurred, to say the least. At this point, I'm in such a state of panic that even I can't quite decipher it.

We drive to a park by the water. It's cold and gusty outside. We walk around in the wind not saying much. I feel a lot of pressure to somehow make our time together amazing since it could be one of the last days before I'm hauled off to prison, or before one of us has a bullet in our heads, but all that pressure just makes me nervous and quiet. When we grow tired of walking, we sit down on some swings and I wonder if the swing will break beneath Tiff's weight but I don't say that. "It's weird," Tiff says, "I feel like we haven't really talked in years. Like we talk, sometimes I guess, but we don't really say anything."

"Well, what do you want to say?"

She shrugs. "I don't know. I guess I've just noticed that, as people get older, they do that more and more: talk without saying anything."

I kick my feet into the snowy ground and swing a little. "Yeah, I've noticed that too."

"You were going to tell me something about someone named Timmy."

I smile to myself. I liked hearing his name. For a moment, his name wasn't synonymous with sadness, wasn't all tangled up in his tragic death. It was just his name. "Timmy was my best friend growing up."

"Do you still keep in touch?"

"He died when I was young."

"Oh... sorry. What did you want to tell me about him?"

"I'm not really sure, actually. Maybe I just wanted to say his name again."

"Alright."

We're silent for a while. "Do you like your friends, Tiff?"

"What do you mean?"

"I mean, you think Caroline threw blood-red paint up at your window. That doesn't seem like a friend to me. I'm sorry, Tiff, but I really don't like her. You know that. I don't think she's a good influence on you. If I'm being honest, I don't really think any of your friends are good influences on you. They're dumb, Tiff. Disrespectful. Do you even like them?"

"I don't know. Sort of. Honestly, I think I'm just their DUFF."

"What's a DUFF?"

"A Designated Ugly Fat Friend."

"God, Tiff, I—"

"And the funniest thing is, I'm kind of scared to lose weight."

"What do you mean?"

"I mean, like... well, being fat, it's... it's all I've ever known really. And I know it's why I'm so unhappy and I guess I'm afraid that if I work really hard and lose all the weight, I might discover that I'm still unhappy. That it doesn't really change anything. Like my friends, they're pretty, so pretty, and yet they—"

"Suck."

She smiles a little. "I was going to say still get upset about things."

"Well, that's cuz they're spoiled, skinny brats. You're smart. You're so much smarter than them, Tiff. I wish you'd wake up and see it."

"See what?"

"That you're a blank slate, kiddo. That you've got your whole life ahead of you."

"You're only like forty, dad. You're a blank slate too."

I shake my head. "I've got blood all over my slate, kiddo. My slate looks a lot like your window."

"What's that supposed to mean?"

I puff air out of my cheeks. "Timmy, it's... it's my fault that he died."

"How?"

My stomach is in knots, but I want to tell her about Timmy because Timmy is the one part of all this that I can tell her about. I need to free something.

"Well, Timmy had a pretty sad life, but the thing about Timmy was he was hardly ever sad. He was a miracle really. He was so smart. You wouldn't have believed this kid. He knew everything. Everything about everything. He probably would have grown up to be a scientist or something. He said he wanted to be an astronaut, and you know what, I think he would have done it. I think he would have gone to space, that's how smart this guy was. And nice. He was the nicest kid you've ever met.

There wasn't a single selfish bone in this kid's body. He was made of magic, Tiff. I swear it."

"So what happened?"

"I was having a bad day. The worst day. I saw Timmy and I took my anger out on him. I said some terrible things. A little later, I went over to his house to apologize but he was gone."

"What do you mean, gone?"

"He... he'd hung himself from his bedroom ceiling," I say, my throat tight. "By the time his mother and I got in there, got him down, it was too late. He was gone."

Tiff lays a hand on my arm. "Oh, dad. Does mom know?"

I wipe my tears on the back of my hand. I'm a jittery mess. "No... I met her a little while after he died and back then, I swore to never speak of him. I haven't said his name in over twenty-five years."

"Well thanks for telling me, dad. I'm sorry. That must be very hard to live with."

"It is." I look out at the water. "Thanks for not making fun of me."

"For what?"

"For crying."

"Why would I make fun of you for crying?"

"I don't know. But thanks anyway."

Twenty-Six

If I can manage to have Tiff survive this whole Max Adams mess, I really hope she has some nice memories of me. That's what I'm thinking while I'm taking a shower that night, while I'm washing my barely-there hair. I hope that when Max Adams hauls me off to prison—or puts me in the ground—Tiffany splits me in two, like how the two roads diverged in that famous poem. I hope she remembers Rex Constanzo, her dad, as a whole different person than Rex Constanzo, the murderer. I hope she knows that the monster who killed Olivia wasn't really a monster at all, just someone who was very, very sad, with a darkness inside that grew like fire, like fever, until he just snapped.

After Tiff and I got home from the park, I took out a ladder, and the strongest cleaning solution I could find beneath the kitchen sink and went up to Tiff's window. Sure enough, it wasn't red paint. Paint would have dried, and this stuff came off with little effort. It was blood.

Our neighbor, Marty, who is annoying, happened to be walking by when I was sponging it off. "What happened here?" he asked, walking up our driveway.

I gritted my teeth. I hated how Marty thought it was acceptable to just walk up our driveway uninvited. He does it a lot when I'm outside pulling weeds or shoveling snow, just looking for someone to talk to. "A stupid prank," I said. "Teenagers, gotta love 'em."

"That's why I never had kids," Marty said with a smile, his hands dug deep in his pockets. "Cuz I knew one day they'd become teenagers."

"The cancer of the earth is what I always say."

"Amen to that." Marty moved closer to the ladder and squinted up at Tiff's bloody window. "You know, this seems a bit far, even for teenagers. When we were kids, sure, we would egg someone's car, toilet paper a house maybe, but that's just downright creepy. Seems like some *Dateline*-level shit to me."

"No kidding."

"Speaking of *Dateline*, you still following that little girl's case, the architect's daughter?"

My stomach churned. "Yeah, I think just about everyone in the tri-state area is. Maybe the whole U.S."

"Chilling stuff, isn't it? Probably a teenager who set that trap. Some sick, twisted little school shooter type who did it just cuz he was bored. It's so sick. It's all so sick. I blame video games. They're so violent. Why do they have to be so violent?"

"I don't know."

"Don't you agree, Rex?"

"I think it takes a lot more than a video game to turn someone into a murderer."

"What does it take, then?"

"Something traumatic, I think. I would guess."

Marty cupped his chin. "Yeah, I don't know. Well, I better get going. Happy cleaning."

He walked away. I didn't stop scrubbing until the window was as spotless as the day it was installed, but after I'd climbed off the ladder and put everything away—as though it never even happened—I noticed the blood caked beneath my fingernails.

Twenty-Seven

For the next three nights, I stay outside with my gun, just in case Max Adams is in the mood to gift us any more snacks or severed animal heads. Each night, when Tiff and Ang are fast asleep, I tiptoe downstairs, put on my winter coat, and sit out on our porch rocking chair, careful not to let it creak.

Sitting out here, I think an awful lot about Timmy. I picture him looking down at me through his telescope from some sort of heaven, or from space, and just shaking his head. He tried to tell me. All those years ago, he tried to tell me all about hot potatoes and how hating only hurts, and I didn't listen. And now here I was, a child murderer, red-eyed and Red Bulled, with a pistol on my knee. I've been relegated to something less than human, a savage beast that wears my pock-marked skin. My eyes have that feral, Max Adams quality to them now. We're alike in so many ways, Max and I, both completely consumed by our anger, caught in the crossfire of our entangled pasts, passing that scalding hot potato back and forth, back and forth, back and forth. It was so futile, comical even.

I know this isn't sustainable, staying up all night like this. I'm growing delirious. I'll have to figure something else out.

Tomorrow, I'll get a surveillance system, or maybe set a tripwire in the front yard. A tripwire. Now there's an idea. I could attach a bell to it, so if I fell asleep in the rocking chair it would wake me up, and then I could shoot Max Adams right between the eyes like stunned cattle, drown the pieces of his chopped-up body in Lake Michigan.

Except I can't shoot Max Adams. My gun doesn't have a silencer or anything. The sound of the gunshot would make Tiff and Ang run downstairs, and would definitely wake up Marty and our other neighbors. And I can't buy a silencer because then there would be purchase records. A gun silencer isn't exactly the kind of thing you can buy at a thrift store. I guess I could get one illegally, from someone on Craigslist or something, but I don't want anyone else on earth to know about all this. Fuck. I've been sitting out here for three nights with nothing but a gun to protect me, and I hadn't even thought it all through.

I'll have to stab Max Adams. I'll have to stab him to death. What other choice do I have? It's either that or wake up to find Tiff's decapitated head on a post just like that pig's, or in bed with me and Ang, like that horse head in *The Godfather*. There's no way I could get away with setting another booby trap. It would be in our front yard for God's sake, everyone would see it.

I'll have to wait for Max Adams to set off the tripwire bell in the middle of the night, leap up from the rocking chair and stab him to death. Except Max Adams is strong. Like Marvel movie strong. What If I stab him in the wrong place? What if I miss all of his vital organs and he just pulls out the knife from his side like it's no bigger than a barroom dart and proceeds to stab me? I'm no match for Max Adams. I'm so soft and squishy. He'd finish me off in a minute. I need something bigger, something that would cover a lot more surface area than a knife. What I need is an axe. Then I could go all *The Shining* on his rapist ass. I start getting a little excited.

So, here's the thing: after accidentally killing Olivia, I felt like the rottenest bastard in the world, and I still do, of course, I do, and after she died, I was content with the idea of leaving Max in peace. He's suffered enough. But has he? Has he really? Who's to say that I'm the only person he's raped? Maybe he rapes that beautiful wife of his. Maybe he rapes his own son. How would I know? It's a sick world out there! Didn't I enter into this whole mess to carry out a bit of justice? To eradicate evil? Seeing Max Adams at that gas station wasn't a coincidence. It was cosmic. Ordained.

Fate.

And here I've gone and lost sight of the whole thing, the whole point. Olivia was nothing but an unfortunate—a deeply unfortunate—casualty in a war I never wanted, a war Max Adams started the day he followed me into the forest and changed everything forever. Every war fought in history has had casualties—collectively, millions of casualties, women and children included—and yet we've fought them just the same. Because we feel it's our duty, our divine requisition and this is mine: I have been called to kill Max Adams, summoned like a sleeper agent out of a fog and into the light. None of this is my fault.

I'm no longer alone. Sitting in this rocking chair, I'm no longer alone. It isn't just me and my gun anymore. I'm surrounded by beings. Celestial beings. They bathe me in holy light. I can give it all to them, all the pain, all the hate and hurt and love and despair. I can give it all to them. I no longer have to carry it.

Tears flow from my eyes. Out of the dark, an angel emerges. Her hair is long, golden. Her eyes are blue.

"It's called a pig roast," she says.

Then I wake up.

Twenty-Eight

Thank God I'd had enough sense to set a 5 a.m. alarm on my phone, just in case I fell asleep outside, so I could get myself back in bed before Tiff and Ang woke up. I wake up on the porch deck, sprawled out on the floor in front of the rocking chair. I have a blinding headache. I get up, open the front door, and walk quietly back inside. I take off my coat. I can't tell if sleep deprivation feels more like being drunk or hungover, I only know that it's hell.

I go upstairs, into our bedroom, and hide my gun beneath my side of the mattress. I climb beneath the covers and fall into feverish dreaming. I see the golden-haired angel. "It's called a pig roast," she says again. Her lips are plump and pink. I see her walking away, down the porch steps, and into the starless night.

I wake up again to the sound of my six thirty bedside alarm and the feel of Ang stirring beside me, stretching her arms above her head. "God, you're hard to sleep with lately," she says. She yawns. "You were thrashing around again, even talking in your sleep this time."

My heart starts to pound. "Oh yeah?"

"Yeah. You just kept saying, 'give it to me, give it to me!' I think you might have been having a sex dream." She laughs. "You poor, deprived fool."

I sigh in relief. I thought I might have admitted to Olivia's murder or something. "I think I was. What's a guy have to do around here to get a little real-life action?" I say, playing into it, even though real-life action is just about the farthest thing from my mind.

"You gotta take me out for another fancy dinner," Ang says.

"God, woman, you're expensive! I might as well hire a prostitute."

To my surprise, Ang laughs.

We shower, get dressed, eat breakfast with Tiff. Driving the delivery van that day, I almost fall asleep behind the wheel a dozen times. The only thing keeping me awake was busying my mind with trying to decode the dream. I think the dream—the first part of the dream—began as a sort of sleep-deprived hallucination while I was half awake on the porch. But what did a pig roast have to do with Max Adams? Was it just my mind sorting through all the pig stuff? And who was the blonde angel? And why had I kept saying 'give it to me' aloud in my sleep? Give me what?

I turn into a gas station. Not *that* gas station but another. I use the bathroom and get a coffee. Olivia's face flashes upon the gas station store TV as I'm paying, the news anchor droning on about what a tragedy it all is. I cast my eyes down, and that's when I notice the spots of blood all over my snow boots.

"You okay, man?"

I snap my head up. The voice came from the cashier, a pasty-faced twenty-something guy in a baseball cap.

"Fine," I say.

"Well, you handed me two twenties to pay for your coffee. It's only a dollar forty-nine."

"Oh." I take back the two crumpled twenties from the counter and fish a dollar and some change from my pocket. "There you go."

He hands me back a dime. I can't stop thinking about the blood on my boots. I'd been wearing them up on the ladder, while I was scrubbing Tiff's window, but I really don't think any of the bloody water had gotten on them. Besides, I've worn them every day since and never noticed the stains.

I turn to leave. I get back in my van and sip my coffee. I'm tired. So very tired.

I wake up hours later in that parking lot, my coffee spilled all over the passenger seat. It's sunset, the sky aflame through the windshield. For a moment, it's beautiful. Then the worries set in: I missed my deliveries, Max Adams is trying to murder my only daughter... I call my boss to say that I'd driven myself to the hospital because of a tingling in my arm that I had thought was a heart attack. After the call, I drive away—nervous as ever—through the watercolor sky I can no longer see.

Twenty-Nine

I arrive home and park my potato chip van next to my Subaru in the garage. I get out of the van and I'm about to head inside when something catches my eye. Something small and shiny. An icy golden color beneath the fluorescent lights.

Our garage contains one of those giant plastic organizer things made up of bins and drawers and cabinets that takes up the whole front wall. The icy golden thing is lodged between two long cupboard doors within the organizer. It looks like a tiny tuft of hay. My brow creases. I step toward it. I reach out and touch it. It's hair. Blonde hair. I crack open the cupboard door.

Something with weight, a lot of weight falls against the inside of the cupboards. I have to lean my own weight against it to keep it from toppling to the floor. More blonde hair spills from the crack between the cupboards like light from a window, caked with dried blood. Then, a fraction of a face. Full, pale lips. A small, upturned nose. It's such a pretty face. A face I know.

I clasp a quivering hand to my mouth. It's Tiff's friend Caroline's face. Caroline's dead, beautiful face. The angel. Caroline's the angel from the dream. Or the half-dream. But why is she dead? Why the *fuck* is she dead?

It all floods back to me. Foggy at first, then clear, like sediment settling to the bottom of a lake.

I remember Caroline's car pulling up to our driveway in the dead of night. She was drunk. She could barely walk a straight line up to our porch. "Mr. Constanzo," she slurred, her spit flying every which way. "Why are you sitting outside? It's two in the morning."

"What are you doing here?"

"I need to talk to Tiffany. To your whore daughter, Tiffany."

"Excuse me?" I stood up. My gun fell from my knee to the floor with a fat slap. For fuck's sake, Caroline had startled me so much that I'd completely forgotten about the fact that I'd had a gun on my knee. I'd been holding onto reality by a single shard.

"Holy shit!" Caroline said. She giggled. "I didn't even see it!" In one swift movement, she knelt down and grabbed the gun. "You have a gun, Mr. Constanzo? You're badass! I thought you were as square as they come. I'm kind of impressed." She pointed the gun right at me.

My heart raced. I lifted my hands in surrender. "Caroline. Put down the gun. Please. You're drunk, sweetie. You're really drunk. I can call you a taxi if you don't want me to call your parents. But you need to hand me that gun."

She laughed again. The laugh was sonorous, well-rehearsed. Sexy. It was a laugh she must have practiced a thousand times before, a laugh that made men and women and boys and girls and the whole entire world fall at her feet. Caroline was beautiful. Dizzyingly beautiful. Tiff's other skinny, slutty friends were nothing but Caroline's lowly serfs, and she, their bottle-blonde queen.

Much to my dismay, Caroline and Tiff had been good friends for a couple of years now. I didn't like it, didn't like *her*, and Caroline knew it. When I heard Tiff and Caroline were fighting, I secretly prayed it would be the end of their friendship. The last thing I wanted was for Tiff to become anything like her. Tiff was sweet, innocent. Caroline was a scantily-clad, attention-seeking pain in the ass. A Gen-Z nightmare.

Caroline flicked her long hair back seductively, the gun still aimed at my forehead. It's like she'd thought she was one of *Charlie's Angels*. "What are you going to do about it, Mr. Constanzo?" she asked, her eyes doe-wide. "Are you going to punish me?" She placed a suggestive lilt on the word punish. She laughed again. It was like she was teasing me. *Flirting* with me. It wasn't the first time I'd felt that Caroline and I had this fucked up, *American Beauty* thing going on between us.

I'm not under the illusion that she actually found me attractive, or that I'm in any way special. I'm sure she put on this act with all of her friend's fathers, lingering in the kitchen to ask them about their boring ass adult lives and listening with such zeal you'd think they were secret agents recounting every death-defying detail of their last mission.

Caroline had a knack for making men feel important. Special. She was beholden to the power generated by their lingering looks and the quick, illicit peaks at her tanned, smooth legs and braless breasts beneath the lacy nightgowns she wore at sleepovers. It was depraved, disturbing... hot. God, Caroline was hot. I know that's fucked up, but Caroline got held back a year. She was nineteen, so me finding her attractive wasn't that immoral. It was normal, actually. Incredibly normal. I'm a man for God's sake, a fact my fat, sexless wife has almost entirely beaten out of me.

Caroline set the gun down on the arm of the rocking chair. I let out a sigh of relief. I quickly stashed the gun in my coat pocket. She laughed for a good ten seconds. "My God," she said. "You should have seen your face. You were so scared. It was priceless. Almost as scared as you were when you saw that pig's head. I was watching you, you know. I was still hiding in the front yard when you walked outside. You ruined everything, Mr. Constanzo. That pig's head was a present... a present for Tiffany. And because of you, she never got to see it. It's sad, really. Our butcher charged me a lot for it."

"None of this is funny, Caroline," I said, my mind spinning around the shock of the pig's head not being from Max Adams. I'd process that later. Right now, I had a very mean, dramatic drunk girl to get the hell off my property. God, this was strange. What a night. Before Caroline came by, everything had been fuzzy, hazy, not quite real. But Caroline's visit was quickly sobering me up, snapping me back into place. "Please, just stay here and let me call you a taxi," I said. I took my cell phone from my pocket to search for a taxi number.

"Not before I talk to Tiff. Could you wake her up for me? I'll wait here."

"It's not the time, Caroline. I know you girls are fighting, but I'm sure it's nothing you can't work out at school tomorrow. I'm sure you girls will forget all about whatever this fight is about in no time."

She scoffed, rolled her eyes. "If only you knew."

"Knew what?"

"Who Tiffany really is."

"I know who she is."

"Oh yeah? Who is she then?"

"She's a good girl. A nice girl. She's nothing like you." The last part just fell from my lips. I couldn't help myself. It felt good to say aloud. Right. I decided that I more than disliked Caroline; I detested her.

Caroline threw her head back laughing. "My God, Mr. Constanzo. That really cracks me up."

"Caroline. Please sit down in that chair. I'm going to call you a taxi." I took her gently by the arm.

"Don't put your hands on me!" she said. "I'll scream, Mr. Constanzo. I'll wake up the whole neighborhood, tell everyone you were getting handsy with me. Tell everyone you *touched* me. I can end you, Mr. Constanzo. Just like I can end Tiffany. Try me."

Fuck. Tiff was right. Teenage girls really could be sociopathic. "Caroline, you need to leave. I'm going to call you a taxi. Or maybe a doctor. I'm not trying to be offensive, but do you have bipolar disorder, Caroline? If you do, Tiff never told me. Is this an episode? That could explain—"

"God! I'm not bipolar!" She laughed like it was the funniest thing she'd ever heard. "To be perfectly honest with you, Mr. Constanzo, I've had... a lot of alcohol tonight, and maybe a little cocaine. So that could be the reason behind all the theatrics, I suppose. But that's not why I'm angry. You should ask your daughter. You should ask her why I'm angry. She'll never tell you the truth, though. So I will. It's called a pig roast. It's called a pig roast, Mr. Constanzo. You can Google it. You'll be amazed at what you find."

"What are you talking about? What the hell is a pig roast?"

"You really want to know? Because once you know, you'll never look at Tiff the same way again. I mean, I know I can't." She narrowed her eyes, smiled. I'd seen that same smug, sinful look in Max Adams' eyes back in his bullying days. This was her moment. The time of her life. This was all some weird play, and she was the star. I could almost see her name in lights, strung up over her head in the night sky. *The Caroline Show.*

"I really want to know," I said. "What the hell is a pig roast?"

"Alright, Mr. Constanzo, I'll tell you. But remember: you asked, so I'm going to give it to you straight, alright? So, not too long ago, I threw a party. At the party, my boyfriend Chad and I were sitting on the couch in my basement. Tiffany was standing in the corner with no one to talk to. It was so sad. The rest of our girlfriends were off hooking up with guys in other rooms and you know why? Because they're hot. Because they're not whales like Tiffany. Sorry, but it's true. At one point, we were watching Tiff standing there alone and Chad said to me 'how hilarious

122

would it be if I tried to fu– sleep with Tiffany tonight?' And then our friend Miles who was also sitting on the couch said, 'how much you wanna bet that she's so lonely and'—sorry, I'm just quoting them here—'fugly that she'd let us both have sex with her at the same time?' And even though I thought it was just a joke, I got mad at them. I'm not the monster you think I am, Mr. Constanzo. I cared about Tiffany. I was her friend. I didn't like them making fun of her and I told them that. I left the couch all mad and then hours went by and I was just enjoying the party and dancing with my friends when I got this message on my phone. It was from Miles. He'd sent me a video. So I pressed play. At first, I didn't know what I was looking at. I knew it was my bedroom, but it was pretty dark. I could see this dark figure on all fours on my bed like a fat, porky pig. And Chad, he was having sex with her from one end, and Miles was having sex with her from the other. It's called a pig roast, because it's like how a stick goes right through a dead pig's mouth and, well, you know, the other end. See, the name makes a lot of sense, right Mr. Constanzo?"

I ran both hands down my face. I was going to be sick. "Where's the video?"

Caroline did that doe-eyed, excessive blinking thing again. "What?" she asked, cocking her head.

"You said there was a video, Caroline. Where is it? For God's sake, a video like that could ruin Tiffany's life!" My blood was boiling. I wanted to kill Caroline right there on that porch. I wanted to step forward and wring her neck.

"Yeah, I know that video could ruin Tiff's life. I'm well aware. But if I release that video, Tiff wouldn't be the only laughing stock of our school. I would be too. So would Miles. So would my boyfriend, who *cheated* on me with Tiffany Constanzo. It's humiliating. For all of us. I don't know what Chad and Miles were thinking. I guess they were really high but... look I know you think I'm a bitch. I know you think I'm like some psychotic fucking bitch but like I told you, I'm drunk and I'm high and I'm really mad. I'm just really fucking mad because I thought Tiff was my friend, and I guess I want you to be mad at her, *disgusted* with her too. I thought she was one of my best friends, Mr. Constanzo, and then she had fat, disgusting sex with my boyfriend. *My* boyfriend. Who the fuck does that? Why the fuck would she do that to me?" For a moment, Caroline looked human. She looked kind. Decent. Maybe we're all decent until the world fucks with us enough. "I loved her, Mr. Constanzo. I loved her, and she betrayed me. Why would she betray me?"

"Caroline... how can I trust that you won't post that video?"

"Because of the reasons I just said! I'm not lying! As you can see, I kind of have a thing for telling the truth. Down to every last gory, disgusting detail." She shuddered. "God, just thinking about it gives me the fucking creeps."

"Was it consensual, Caroline?"

"What?"

"The sex, Caroline."

"I think so."

My eyes bulged. "You *think* so?"

124

"I wasn't there. I don't know. The guys were drunk. Tiffany was drunk too. When I went to find them in my bedroom, the room was empty. It wasn't a live video. Tiff had left the party long before."

"Jesus. Jesus Christ." I paced around the porch and tried to breathe. "Did you get rid of the video?"

"Miles got rid of the video. Chad doesn't know there's a video at all. If Chad knew that Miles had filmed him cheating on me and then sent it to me, well, Chad would never talk to him again. Miles made me swear to delete my copy. And I told him I did but I... I didn't." She giggled, flashed that sickly smile once more. She was done looking weak, appearing human. She'd hated it. *The Caroline Show* was back from intermission. "So you see, Mr. Constanzo, I love Chad, I really do, but statistically speaking, most high school relationships don't pan out and now that I know that Chad's a cheater, I think I'd like to hold onto the video for a little while, sit on it, for when I find out he's cheated on me with someone a hell of a lot hotter than Tiffany, someone that could actually make me jealous. Then maybe I'll release the video. Or maybe I won't. I probably won't." She winked, like some sort of movie villain.

"Caroline, you're not leaving until you delete the video, and somehow prove to me that you don't have any other copies."

"Mr. Constanzo! Keeping me here against my will? I think they have a word for that. Oh yeah, it's kidnapping." She turned to leave. "Tell Tiffany I say hi. Did she tell you about all the pork rinds I stuffed in her locker last week? You should have seen her face when they spilled out into the hallway. It was priceless. Tell her I can't wait to see her at school tomorrow. We've been having a lot of fun at school, Tiff and me," she said over her shoulder, her blonde hair bouncing behind her.

"Caroline! Get back here!" I followed her and gripped her arm again, harder this time. "Give me your phone."

"No."

"Give it to me!"

She spat right in my face. "No!"

I set my jaw, which was now sopping with saliva. It took everything in me not to slap her. I stuck my hand into her pocket and tried to fish out her phone, but her jeans were so skin tight that my hand was in her pocket a lot longer than it should have been. "Rape!" she screamed, loudly enough to wake the neighbors if she kept at it. Loudly enough to wake Ang and Tiffany. "Rape!" I pulled my hand from her pocket and held it over her mouth.

"Shut the fuck up," I said, my other hand trying to hold her arms behind her back. She freed them, and tore my hand from her mouth.

"Rape!" she screamed again, somehow even louder this time. I didn't know what to do. I got my hand over her mouth again and my other arm around her waist holding her arms down. I started dragging her away from the porch, past the driveway and to the bushes at the side of the house. I led us halfway inside the bushes. "Now you listen to me," I said in her ear. "If you scream again, I'll have no other choice but to knock you out and take your phone. You don't want that, Caroline. Trust me. Now calmly, I want you to take out your phone, show me where the video file is, and delete it."

She couldn't talk beneath the heavy press of my hand but she nodded her compliance. With a deep breath, I let her go. She spun around to look at me, to show me her slow-moving smile. "Rape!" she screamed again, at the top of her lungs. "Rape!"

I grabbed her by the neck, and banged her head against the house's brick exterior. Hard. I never meant for it be so hard. I did it just to knock her out for maybe a minute, just to shut her up, but her head landed with far too heavy of a thwack. Her body went limp. I could first feel the change in her neck, no longer corded but soft, resigned.

"Caroline," I said. I jostled her neck, as though I could will life back into it. My heart pumped panic to my every extremity. "Caroline."

Her face was dull, dummy-like, her lips parted yet devoid of breath. I shook her shoulders. I cried out helplessly. "Caroline."

I laid her body down on the driveway. Her eyes were open, staring vacantly at the sky.

I started to cry. It was painful, tight, like a fire burning in my chest. I couldn't stop crying.

Blood began to blossom behind her head, like a rose borne from moonlit pavement.

Thirty

"Dinner's ready," Ang says as I open the garage door to the house. I'm shaky, nauseous. I'd just moved Caroline's body from the cupboards to the trunk of my Subaru.

I walk in. Ang is standing in the kitchen with an apron on. The table is set. The room smells of roast beef. "Long day?" she asks when I don't say anything.

"Huh?"

"Are you alright?"

"What? Yeah. Fine."

"You're so pale, Rex. You look sick. Are you sure you're alright?" I lose my footing. The kitchen spins on its axis like a classroom globe. "Oh my God! Rex!" I open my eyes. I'm lying on the kitchen floor. I've bumped my head. It's killing me. Ang is sitting over me, shaking my shoulders just like I'd shaken Caroline's last night. "My God, Rex! You fainted. Are you alright?"

I blink. "Yeah. I think so."

"Come. Come lie down on the couch." Ang pulls me up. I place a hand to the back of my throbbing head. We waddle toward the living room couch, her arm beneath my arm. I lie down. "I'll get you some water," Ang says. She goes into the kitchen, returns. "Here you go." She sits down beside my shoulder on the couch. She passes me the glass. I take a small sip. "God, Rex, I thought you were dead," Ang says. "I thought you'd died right there in the kitchen." She starts to cry. It's sad, but I'm really surprised she cares enough to cry. "It's crazy, isn't it?" she says. "How it can all end so fast. In the blink of an eye." She's really crying now, her eyes two tiny swimming pools. It makes my heart swell.

"Where did you go, Ang?" I say, reaching up to touch her hair.

"What?"

"Years ago, it's like you turned off. I don't know where you went. I've been here waiting, just waiting for you to come back. I've been so lonely, Ang. I've never felt so alone."

"Oh, Rex." She kisses me on the forehead, my cheek, my mouth. It's so sweet. So achingly sweet. The most genuine affection she's shown me in years. This pure kind of affection that reminds me immediately of Lars.

A few months after Max Adams raped me, I got this haircut. A new salon had opened in town, and this rich kid from school, Will, he'd gotten a really great haircut there. Elvis Presley cool. I thought that maybe if I got a new look or something, started dressing differently, get those better jeans like my sister told me to, it would help me become somebody new. Would help me forget.

I walked into the salon. I felt out of place. I'd only been to cheap barber shops before, but I'd been saving up my paper route money for an appointment. I'd told my parents I was going to our usual barber, Tony. My dad would have called me a fag if he knew I was going to a salon.

In the salon stood a wiry middle-aged man with a warm smile. He introduced himself as Lars. He was from Austria. He had the nicest accent. We talked a lot while he washed my hair. We talked about all kinds of things. He asked me all about my life, about school, and what I liked to do. For once, I felt important.

At one point, he stepped away to get a different pair of scissors while he was cutting my hair. Then his cold hand pressed the back of my neck. I bristled, jerked away. For a moment, I hadn't realized it was Lars. Tears flooded my eyes. "I'm sorry," I said. I was mortified. "I'm so sorry. You scared me. You startled me, that's all." Since the rape, I'd been scared like that twice before. Once with my sister. Another time with a teacher.

"It's okay," Lars said. He rubbed my shoulder with that same hand. It didn't feel so cold anymore. "You're okay, you're alright."

"I'm sorry. I'm so sorry." I patted my eyes down. "God, this is embarrassing. I don't know why I'm crying. This—"

"Don't apologize. Everybody cries, Rex. Come to think of it, I cried just last week."

"Really?" He kept rubbing my shoulder in a fatherly way. It felt nice. Gentle. I never wanted it to end.

"Yes, really. I lost my wife just last year. I cried at her grave."

"I'm sorry. That... that's awful."

He opened the scissors and started trimming the back of

my hair. "You're a good boy, Rex. A very good boy. I'm so sorry someone hurt you."

My stomach sloshed around. "What?"

He didn't say anything. He just kept cutting my hair. I hung my head so I didn't have to face myself in the mirror. I shut my eyes tight, tears seeping through. I sat there crying in the barber chair listening to the snip-snip of his scissors.

Thirty-One

"Let's go on a walk, dad, after dinner," Tiff says. She slices into her piece of roast beef, takes a bite.

"Alright," I say, even though I feel like absolute shit. I'm onto my fourth glass of wine, tipsy as anything. I already regret saying yes to that after-dinner walk with Tiffany. I'm having a hard time sitting across from her now that I know what a filthy girl she truly is. I watch her as she eats her roast beef, bits of brown residue stuck into the corners of her mouth, one lone, meaty drop of saliva trekking the length of all three chins, which jiggle as she chews. Her skin is pink with rosacea, puffy, pig-like. She disgusts me.

"You just fainted, Rex. Are you sure that going on a walk is a good idea?" Ang asks.

"Maybe you're right," I say to Ang.

"Come on, dad. We won't go far, I promise," Tiff says. Tiff shovels another fat forkful of food into her mouth, and I notice that her bottom lip is twitching, as though she's trying not to cry.

"Am I invited on this walk?" Ang asks.

Tiff takes a sip of water. "Is it okay if it's just me and dad tonight, mom?"

"Alright," Ang says, smiling.

After dinner, Tiff and I put our coats on and head out the door. We walk down the driveway a little when Tiff grabs my arm. She's crying.

"Tiff, what is it?" I ask.

She's crying so hard she can't speak. "Dad," she finally says. "Dad."

"What, Tiff? What?"

"I... I... I..."

"What?"

"I saw you last night."

I swallow. I swear I can hear my heart beating. "What?"

"I... I heard screaming. So I went downstairs and outside. You were dragging Caroline away from the house. She kept yelling the word 'rape'. You... you slammed her into the wall..." She buries her face in her hands and sobs. "You... you slammed her so hard. I... I must have cried out or something, and you... you snapped your head up. You saw me. You started toward me, and I was so afraid of you, dad." Her chins tremble. "I was so afraid... but then you fainted on the porch. Then you fell asleep. And then I... then I took care of Caroline's body... and all the blood." Her voice cracks. "Because I loved you and I... I didn't understand."

"Tiff. Oh my God, Tiff." I gulp. I reach out to her but she flinches, pulls away. "It was an accident, Tiff. A horrible accident. Caroline, she... she threatened you. She has a video of... of that night. The party. She's a maniac. You know that.

133

She was out of her mind. She... she wouldn't shut up. I was protecting you! For God's sake, I was protecting you! That video could ruin your life. I... I don't understand why... why would you do that, Tiff? Why would you let those boys... what happened, what went—"

She sniffles, wiping her tears on the sleeve of her coat. "All my life, dad, you... you've made me feel like... like nothing. Like less than nothing," she says, staring straight past me. "Lately, you've been so nice to me. It's what I've always wanted. To be seen by you. But then I realized how weak I've been, to just let you back in, to... you asked me why I let those boys do that. Because I wanted to feel pretty. Wanted. Good enough for once. But last night, I saw you for what you really are, for what you've always been: a monster. A fucking monster." Her eyes flicker back to me, shining with tears and burning with contempt. She takes Caroline's glittery pink cellphone from her pocket, which in all my shock and sleep deprivation, I'd managed to completely forget about. Her face crumples. "I'm calling the police, dad," she says, her voice squealy. "I'm turning you in."

I step back. "What?"

She heads for the porch steps. I take her by the arm. "You fat, fucking whore!" I scream right into her ear, loud enough to shatter her eardrum and I hope I do. I slap her. I slap her right across her fat, fucking face. "I did this for you. I did this all for you! You ungrateful fucking whore!"

The front door flies open. "What's going on?" Ang asks, her face ashen.

I throw Tiff down on the snow. She sits there on her porky ass crying her eyes out. I run up the porch steps, push past Ang and enter the house. I grab my coat, my wallet, my Subaru keys. I cross the hallway to the garage. I get in my Subaru, open the garage door.

I drive right past Tiff and over to Ang. I roll my window down, look into Ang's big empty eyes. I guess this is goodbye.

"You should have let me wash your hair," I tell her. "Months ago, I asked you if I could wash your hair and you said no. Why'd you say no? I just wanted to wash my wife's goddamn hair!"

I roll the window back up and speed away.

Thirty-Two

I drive right to the Adams' suburb. It's 8 p.m. Time for Max Adams' run.

Like clockwork, the front door opens to the Adams' beautiful house. Max Adams runs down the driveway in black running wear. He's got his fluorescent armbands around his biceps so drivers don't run him over. I laugh at the cosmic symmetry of it all.

I gun the car. I smile, wickedly. It's perfect, this ending. My final act. My swan song.

Let me burn out in a burst of light. Let the stars sing my name. Let me go out with a—

BANG!

Max Adams' body hurls itself over the hood of my car. There's blood on the windshield, bits of hair, brain pieces. His body rolls from the hood onto the road. I run him over. Thump, thump, thump go the tires over his shoulders, his back... crack goes his skull. I back up, do it all over again. I roll my window down to hear it better. Thump, thump, thump. Thumpety, thump, thump, thump.

I take off, stealing a glance at Max Adams' mangled body in the rearview mirror. I start to laugh. Tears roll down my face.

The streetlights shimmer their goodbye as Max Adams' soul descends to hell, swallowed up by asphalt and dragged into a forest of fire below.

I speed down Max Adams' suburb street and onto the highway. I stop at a dive bar. It's a country bar and country music is playing. "What can I get ya?" the bartender asks.

"Whisky!" I say. I slap my knee. I laugh my head off.

"What's funny?" he asks.

"Well, I don't know, partner," I say, looking around the near empty room. "Just about everything, I guess." He gives me a weird look, pours the whisky. I down it in two gulps. I ask for more. I drink it. I feel warm. Whole. "You seem like a good guy," I say. I'm drunk now. "How would you like to solve the state's hottest crime? How'd you like to be a hero?"

He gives me the same weird look. "I think you've had a bit too much," he says.

"I'm serious! How'd you like to live and die a hero? A true hero? Isn't that what everyone wants, partner? To live and die a hero? To do something? Anything? To just do something? I've got this wife, she... she's not going to speak to me anymore after tonight. It's over. But she... she... it's like she switched off. Years ago. It's like she switched off. You know what she reminds me of, partner? She reminds me of a toy, an action figure, or something like that, with a switch on its back. And that switch... it's switched off. She's like a dead fish. Like some dead fish. All I want to do is love her, and she won't let me. I have so much love to give. Sometimes, I want to shake her shoulders.

I want to just shake her shoulders and scream 'Do something! Do something, Ang! Anything! Run, scream, cry. Jump around! Just do something, anything!' She pushes everything down. All her natural urges, her instincts. I used to be that way too. I used to push everything down too. But not anymore. Do you ever feel that way, partner? Like you push things down?"

He sighs, staring down at the rag he's got in his hand, turning slow, sudsy circles along the bar counter. "This is America," he says. "Everyone pushes things down."

"But it doesn't have to be that way! Look, do you remember when you were young, when you were a kid, and you'd see a girl you liked at school and you'd get a boner? You couldn't help it, and then you'd have to hide your boner behind your textbook, or flip it up under your pants? Sorry to be crass like this, but it's important. What I'm getting at is important. And I'll get to it. Don't you worry. I'm not wasting any of your time, partner. I've got a surprise for you. One hell of a surprise. Anyways. Do you remember when you wanted things? Do you remember what it was like to be young and full of lust and love and how you could feel the blood rushing through your veins, through your cock? The way you wanted to drink a girl's spit, wear her skin, drown her in your cum? The kind of all-consuming love that felt like you'd died? I want that again, partner. Don't you? Don't you want to just do what you want? For once, just do whatever the fuck you want? No limits, no consequences. Just living your life on your terms. Just living out the wild circus of it all."

His cheeks are red. He's still staring down at that rag in his hand. "Uh... sure," he says. "I don't know."

I lean forward a little so he does too. "What if I told you I've got a dead girl in the trunk of my car? What if I told you that, last night, I bashed her head into a wall? You see, this girl, Caroline, she was the cancer of the earth. You wouldn't have believed how this girl talked to people, even parents. She was rude as anything. Gen-Z... Gen-Z will bring on Armageddon, I swear it. You mark my words, partner. I wish you could have met this girl, Caroline. You wouldn't have believed a girl like her existed. She was so rude. Mean. She was a real good-for-nothing whore." I laugh, lift my empty whisky glass. "Pour me another, partner! I'm having a good time, a real good time!"

He sighs, pours me another glass. I drink it. I wait for him to react, to call the police or something. My eyes wander around the room, around all the dart boards and pool tables. "You don't believe me?" I say. "You don't believe that I've got a dead girl in the trunk of my car? I can show you if you'd like."

The bartender laughs. "Buddy, if I had a dollar for every drunk joe that sat on that stool and told me he'd committed some crazy crime or fucked ten girls at once, or fucking went to Mars and back, I sure as hell wouldn't be cleaning up this bar counter right now. I'd be in a castle in Europe, fucking a French girl."

I smile big. "You don't believe me!" I laugh. "God, that's hilarious. You don't believe me!" I slap my knee again, once, twice, three times. I'm winded. "Everyone wants to be someone, don't they? Everyone wants to do something, something big. And see,

I did, I did something big tonight. I'm a somebody now. The hero of my own life. I'll tell you what I did tonight, partner, because we're friends. Because pretty soon I'm going to be rotting in a prison cell for the rest of my life. I killed Max Adams, partner. The guy with the dead daughter. I killed that guy and I killed his daughter too."

The bartender creases his brow. "I know that name. Max Adams."

"From the news. The guy with the dead daughter."

"What?"

"The little girl! The one who's on the news every goddamned day. The architect's daughter. I killed her. I killed her because her dad—that pretty boy architect—raped me. Back in school. Max Adams raped me." I clasp a hand to my mouth. "Oh my God, I've said it!" Tears fill my eyes. "I was raped by Max Adams out in the woods when I'd just turned sixteen. I was out in the woods—"

"The woods!" The bartender's eyes go wide. "That's how I know the name. Max Adams. Max Adams was that kid who was killed in the woods. The Boy Without a Face."

"What?"

"The one... the kid... the one who was stabbed with his own pocketknife like a hundred and fifty times. The one who got his face ripped off."

The country music starts getting louder and louder and louder and louder and the bar keeps getting smaller. I'm afraid the walls will crush me. "What do you mean? Max Adams, he... he's the architect. The one with the dead daughter."

The bartender creases up his brow some more. "No, that guy's name is Henry."

I give myself a good ol' slap on the forehead like *you idiot!* "Yeah, oh yeah. I forgot to tell you. He... he changed his name. To escape his past, I guess. Max Adams was a real nasty kid. The nastiest kid. I mean, he was a goddamn rapist. So, he changed his name. When I saw the name Henry on the news, it surprised me too. But if you knew Max Adams, you'd know why he changed his name. You'd get why he'd had to."

The bartender shakes his head. "You're wrong. Max Adams was killed in the woods decades ago, when he was a teenager. Just left out there stabbed to death without a face. When I was young, kids made a ghost story out of it. Growing up, I went to this summer camp here in Michigan and we kids used to try to scare each other talking about Max Adams' ghost around the campfire. The Boy Without a Face."

"That's nonsense. He's Henry! Max Adams is... *was* Henry!"

"Nope. Nope, he's not. That guy Henry, he looks a lot like Max would have if he'd had the chance to grow up, I'll give you that. The same blue eyes, dark hair. I remember Max's picture from the news. A real handsome kid. Did you live under a rock when you were growing up? How do you not know Max Adams was killed? Everyone in the whole world knows."

"I..."

"The whisky... you're confused, is all. You're talking crazy. Happens to the best of us. Are you okay, though? For real. You look terrible. No more whisky for you. You're cut off."

I push myself up off the bar stool. I fork over some cash to pay for my drinks. I think I gave him a hundred-dollar bill.

I stumble outside, my chest heaving beneath my winter coat, my breath like clouds of cigarette smoke. I throw up all over my blood-stained boots.

How had I not remembered? How had I not known that Max Adams was dead? How had I not seen it on the news? I'd stayed home from school for two weeks after, but that couldn't have hidden it forever. I must have seen it on news specials, overheard it in conversations. I guess my brain must have blocked it out. Buried it.

I take the Subaru keys from my pocket, unlock it and sit in the front seat. The window is still open from when I'd rolled it down to listen to the crunch of Max's—*Henry's*—bones. I look up at the stars. There's a blood moon tonight, half-red in the sky. I think about Max Adams. The real Max Adams. I remember now. I remember everything. The memories fall softly like snow.

I'm back in the woods. Max Adams had just raped me. He was standing over me. I screamed. He whipped out his pocketknife. "Tell anyone about this, Gimpy, and I'll kill your whole family," he said.

I got up, pulled up my pants. I grabbed the rock he used to hit my head and hit his head with it. Hard. It knocked him out. He crumpled to the forest floor like a broken doll. His pocketknife had fallen to the ground beside him. I picked it up. I lifted up his shirt. I drew a line in blood, right along his

142

spine, from the top of his neck to the bottom of his back. I don't know why I did it, but, for a second, it made me forget about the pain.

I kept on drawing those lines, deeper and deeper each time, until I hit bone, burst organs. It was tantric. I was God.

"You kill a deer?"

"Huh?"

An old man stands at my Subaru window. He's just parked his car beside mine. He nods toward the blood and hair and brain pieces on my windshield, on my front bumper. I start to cry. I'm Henry's Max Adams. It's the cruelest truth I've ever known.

"Yeah," I say, unable to look into the old man's eyes. "I guess I did."

Acknowledgements

Thank you, from the bottom of my heart, to Martin and Maggie, for believing in the book, and for working so hard to bring it out into the world.

Thank you to my wonderful family and friends. This is a dark book that not everyone in my life is comfortable being affiliated with, so I'm not naming names, but you know who you are. I am eternally grateful.

www.ingramcontent.com/pod-product-compliance
Ingram Content Group UK Ltd.
Pitfield, Milton Keynes, MK11 3LW, UK
UKHW030657030325
455745UK00008BA/107